IT'S NOT EASY BEING MEAN

Don't miss the Q&A
with Lisi Harrison!
in back of book

IT'S NOT EASY BEING MEAN

A CLIQUE NOVEL BY
LISI HARRISON

LITTLE, BROWN AND COMPANY

New York ᴧ Boston

Little, Brown and Company
Hachette Book Group USA
1271 Avenue of the Americas, New York, NY 10020
Visit our Web site at www.lb-teens.com

First Edition: March 2007

ALLOYENTERTAINMENT   Produced by Alloy Entertainment
                      151 West 26th Street, New York, NY 10001

ISBN-10: 0-316-11505-3
ISBN-13: 978-0-316-11505-6

10 9 8 7 6 5 4 3 2 1
CWO
Printed in the United States of America

For Luke and Bee Bee

CLIQUE novels by Lisi Harrison:

THE CLIQUE

BEST FRIENDS FOR NEVER

REVENGE OF THE WANNABES

INVASION OF THE BOY SNATCHERS

THE PRETTY COMMITTEE STRIKES BACK

DIAL L FOR LOSER

IT'S NOT EASY BEING MEAN

Dylan Marvil pig-pressed her nose against the bay window in Massie Block's bedroom and then craned her neck slightly left toward the gated entrance of the Block estate. "Um, Kuh-laire? You may wanna see this."

Dropping the armload of designer clothes she'd been color-coding for Massie, Claire Lyons scurried to Dylan's side. "What is it?" She pushed up the sleeves on her orange velour hoodie.

"Todd and Tiny Nathan are selling your itchy pink-and-red polka-dot scarf to that fast talker Carrie Randolph."

Alicia Rivera tossed her *Teen Vogue* on the hardwood floor, slid off Massie's fluffy, lavender-scented bed, and wiggled between them. Her black velvet leggings were spotted with purple lint from Massie's bedding. "Ew, that LBR rode her bike all the way over here? To buy *that*?"

"Todd!" Claire shouted at her brother while struggling to unhook the window's iron latch. "Party scarf wasn't on the list!"

Kristen Gregory balanced on her tiptoes, straining to see over their heads. Tiny yellow-and-green Puma shorts showed off her sharp soccer calves, which flexed as she bobbed to witness the unfolding scandal. "How much do you think he's made so far?"

"Too much." Claire pounded on the soundproof glass. "I can't believe people actually want to buy my stuff."

"Me, either," Massie mumbled, refusing to get distracted by the LBRs who suddenly thought Claire's cheap machine washables were worth something because she'd starred in a predictable Hollywood movie with Abby Boyd and Conner Foley. She had more important things to think about.

Turning to her swiveling three-paneled full-length mirror, Massie studied her reflection, wondering if she should have saved today's outfit for tomorrow. Her C&C California black-and-gray-striped V-necked sweater dress exuded confidence over a pair of mint green leggings and gray suede ankle boots. But still, the dress was boxy, and therefore would only know life on Sundays and snow days.

After letting out a long sigh, Massie returned to her life-size mannequin, which ruled the corner of her room between the walk-in closet and her mirror. She fastened a thin gold braided belt around its waist, then stepped back, tilted her head to the left, and took it all in. Cinching the brown Ella Moss T-shirt dress instantly elevated it from a seven to a nine. But still, something was off. Was it the tan linen vest? Too safari? Or maybe it was the espresso-colored Marc Jacobs ballet flats. Yup. It was the flats. They were a little too precious for her first day back at Octavian Country Day School. After her celebrity-studded three-week expulsion, she needed something that said, "I'm back and better than ever." And right now all she had was, "Hey, guys, how's it goin'?" She took a long swig of Tab Energy, then tore the poo-colored clothes off the Massie-quin.

Time to start over.

"Ehmagawd!" Dylan squealed. "It's the pasty goth barista from Starbucks!" She shook her arms free of the long military-style jacket that covered her dark-wash Earnest Sewn pencil-straight jeans, revealing a faded pink Porky Pig tee.

"Buying my Kipling backpack!" Claire wailed. "Monkey and all!"

"Thank Gawd." Alicia rolled up the sleeves on her pin-striped Norma Kamali shirtdress. "That thing was eye-poison."

Kristen's narrow blue eyes widened, "It looks like your books are still in it."

"They *are*!"

"Massie, you have to see this!" Alicia giggled and kicked Dylan's jacket aside.

"Pass." Massie pulled the flats off her mannequin and replaced them with navy Michael Kors cork wedges. "I'm busy."

Besides, she already knew what Claire's stalkers looked like. They had been riding past the estate on bikes and scooters for the last two days to see where the star of the movie *Dial L for Loser* slept, ate, and peed. Massie was constantly fighting the urge to poke her freshly razored layers out the window and yell, "Didn't any of you stalkers watch

The Daily Grind? Didn't you see Alicia and me broadcasting live from the set every day for two weeks straight? Don't you remember those pictures of me with Conner Foley in *Us Weekly*? Why don't you want to buy *my* scarves? Why don't you want to take *my* picture? *Whyyyyyy?*" But all she said was, "Get used to it, Miss I'm-moving-to-California-to-be-a-Hollywood-superstar."

"Why should I get *used* to Todd and Tiny Nathan selling my things to strangers?" Claire pressed her entire left side against the bay window.

"A celebrity's life is public property. If you don't like it . . ." Massie grabbed a thin white remote off her bedside table and pressed her manicured thumbnail into the top right button. "Leave it."

The window clicked open and Claire fell forward.

"Whoa!" She steadied herself on the curved stone ledge.

Massie examined the newly naked mannequin. "Now will you puh-lease focus!"

Finally, everyone turned away from Todd, Tiny Nathan, and the red Radio Flyer wagon filled with Claire's personal belongings. They stood, their backs to the window, while Massie paced.

"In case you forgot, the Pretty Committee was just expelled from OCD for *three* weeks because we ran off into the woods on a class field trip and got lost." Massie put her hands on her narrow hips. "Instead of sitting on our couches watching *High School Musical*, we went to Hollywood and made something of ourselves and—"

"Speak for yourself." Kristen exchanged an eye-roll with Dylan.

"Yeah, some of us weren't *allowed* to go to California, remember?" Dylan stuffed a cube of watermelon-flavored bubble gum in her mouth, then immediately unwrapped another piece and jammed it in.

"Some of us stayed here, wrote a butt-kissing essay, and signed *your* name to it so you could get back into school, re-*mem*-ber?" Kristen glared at Massie.

"Of course I re-*mem*-ber. I was getting to that part," she lied. "But seeing as you already mentioned how great you think you are, I'll skip over it."

Kristen and Dylan muttered apologies.

Massie took a cleansing breath, exhaled in frustration, and continued. "The point is, in less than twenty-four hours we'll be walking the halls at OCD while hundreds of jealous eyeballs scan us, searching for flaws."

"Why would they do that?" Claire scratched her blond eyebrows. "You always say everyone *loves* the Pretty Committee."

"No. I always say they want to *be* us." Massie swatted her flirty new chocolate-colored side part away from her amber eyes. "Which means they're secretly studying us, hoping to spot a weakness so they can—"

"A weakness?"

"Yeah, like an out-of-place hair." Alicia pointed to her perfect side part.

"Or bad grades," Kristen offered.

"Or an open fly." Dylan covered her crotch.

"Or smudged eyeliner, or last year's boots, or peanut-butter breath." Massie circled her hand to show that the list went on and on. "Anything they can use to put *us* down."

"Why would they want to—?"

"It makes them feel better about their sorry selves. That's why."

"Point!" Alicia lifted her finger.

Massie took another swig of Tab Energy and slammed it down on her mirrored pedestal night table. She fell onto her bed beside her ah-dorable sleeping black pug, Bean, allowing herself to get swallowed by the cluster of white faux-fur pillows as if surrendering to an avalanche. "If we don't look ah-mazing times ten, everyone will think the Pretty Committee's lost its magic and we'll be blog food." She lifted her arm out of the fluff and checked her silver DKNY bangle watch. "It's already 4:27 p.m., and not a single outfit has been approved."

"Point!" Alicia plopped down beside her.

Bean lifted her head and growled.

"You're right," Dylan pouted. "Sorry." She joined them on the bed.

Claire turned and closed the window.

"What about the soccer lesson?" Kristen grabbed the white wooden bedpost and stretched a hamstring.

"Ew! Why would we want to spend our last hours of freedom doing *that*?" Alicia shuddered, as if Kristen had suggested using their blush brushes to scrub toilets in the boys' locker room.

"Um, starting tomorrow, you're members of OCD Sirens. Remember?"

They all looked at her blankly.

"Gawd, don't any of you want to learn how to play before you join the team?"

"Opposite of yes." Alicia reached to the floor, picked up her *Teen Vogue,* and crawled under the feathery purple duvet cover.

"Leesh, I swear, if we don't make it to the finals because you—"

"Hey!" Massie stood and held up her palm like a crossing guard. "Kristen, are you mad at Alicia?"

"No, I'm just—"

"Then why does it sound like you want to socc-er?"

Everyone cracked up except Kristen, who folded her arms across her green Juicy hoodie and looked up at Massie's new multicolored crystal chandelier as if begging it to give her strength. "It was *your* decision to join the team."

"We had no choice." Dylan punched the mattress. "It was the only way Principal Burns would let us back into school."

"You had to pick an extracurricular activity," Kristen reminded them. "No one said it had to be soccer."

"We thought it'd be a good way to bond with the boys." Massie twirled the diamond stud in her left earlobe.

"And burn calories." Dylan rubbed her flat stomach like someone who'd eaten too much chocolate-chip cookie dough.

"And tone." Alicia curled into the fetal position.

"Claire, *you* like soccer, right?"

"Yeah, but I have to meet my agent in Manhattan, so I'm gonna miss practice."

Clenching her fists, Massie fought another urge to tear Claire's white-blond hair out of her ah-nnoying, conceited, movie-star head. "Are you seriously going to pass up a summer cohosting pool parties and gossiping about boys to *work*?"

"Um, yeah," Claire said, in a who-wouldn't sort of way.

"Point!" Alicia lifted her finger out from the duvet.

Dylan and Kristen giggled while Massie contemplated her sudden need to make Claire cry. She wanted to hurt her feelings and crush her confidence and treat her like an unworthy, unimportant, undesirable loser. Maybe then Claire would understand how Massie felt, being dumped for a stupid movie.

All of a sudden, a shock of angry boy music filled the room. Massie raced to her silver cube of an alarm clock and slammed the off button. But the electrified screaming wouldn't stop. It sounded like someone had placed a gigantic set of Bose headphones around her alabaster-white walls and cranked up the volume on some basement dweller's amplified nervous breakdown.

"It's coming from outside." Dylan assumed her old position by the bay window. "More fans."

Bean jumped off the bed and barked her way to Dylan's side.

Everyone followed.

"I wonder what they're gonna buy?" Kristen pinched her bottom lip.

"Hopefully Todd." Massie lifted Bean and stroked her ears.

"Ehmagawd!" Alicia covered her highly glossed mouth like a shocked *American Idol* winner. "It's not a fan. It's Skye Hamilton."

"Listening to AFI?" Kristen crinkled her perfect, J-shaped nose.

"Imposs!" Massie marched across her ivory sheepskin area rugs and pushed the girls aside.

"Who is that?" Claire asked, catching her balance on the wall.

"Eighth-grade alpha," Massie explained, her eyes fixed on Skye.

"Check out that yellow Porsche convertible," Kristen ogled.

"Check out the driver." Alicia rolled her shoulders back like she was offering her C-cups to the universe. "I fully heart guys who wear dark jeans with gray tees. And I double fully heart black wavy hair."

"That's the cutest guy I've *never* seen." Dylan sighed.

"*I've* seen him." Kristen fanned her cheeks. "On an Abercrombie bag."

"How does her hair look so good?" Dylan twirled a shiny red ringlet around her finger, then burped. "I'd look all Chuckie from *Rugrats* after a ride in that thing."

"Can you see what she's wearing? Is it dance-y?" Alicia rested her forehead against the windowpane. "Her parents own Body Alive Dance Studio. Not only is she ah-mazing at ballet, modern, jazz, and tap, but she gets whatever she wants from the B.A.D.S. apparel store." A steam puff of envy marred the glass as she sighed. "Can anyone see her legs? I bet she's wearing a leotard, or maybe a unitard."

"Um, you're the only 'tard I see," Massie snapped, refusing to publicize her Skye obsession.

"Why haven't I noticed her before?" Claire asked, poking her head between Massie and Alicia.

"She's always with the boys." Massie tried her best to sound unimpressed. "That's why her group is called the DSL Daters."

"Why?"

"Because they make super-fast connections," she replied flatly, like it should have been obvious.

"Do you think she's here to buy something of mine?" Claire asked, sounding one part shocked and two parts psyched.

"Come awn!" Massie rolled her eyes. "That'd be like Paris Hilton asking Hermione Granger to borrow something for the VMAs."

"Point." Alicia lifted her finger. "She's been a regular at Fashion Week since she was potty trained. I heard she sat beside the Harajuku girls at the L.A.M.B. show this year."

"Con-firmed." Dylan drew a check mark in the air. "My mom saw her there."

"Look!" Alicia giggled. "Todd is giving her Claire's Powerpuff Girls jammies."

The almond biscotti Massie had eaten after lunch pulled a sudden U-turn.

"*No!* Those have a blueberry stain on the butt!" Tiny beads of sweat gathered above Claire's cherry ChapStick–covered lips.

"There's no *way* Skye Hamilton is an FOC," Massie murmured in disbelief.

"A what?" Kristen let out a phlegmy cackle.

Massie lowered Bean into her white miniature four-poster bed, giving the girls a moment to ponder her latest expression. Finally, and with pride, she blurted, "FOC—fan of Claire's."

"I heart that!" Alicia beamed.

"Brill!" Dylan high-fived Massie, who then high-fived Kristen.

"Toddddd!" Claire pressed her clammy palms against the windowpane.

"Wait! Skye is giving the pajamas *back*," Dylan announced like a sportscaster. "Now she's shaking her head and reaching into her stone-colored Juicy Couture Sienna bag, and pulling out . . . a gold envelope. She's handing it to Tiny Nathan . . . no, Todd . . . no, Tiny Nathan . . . no, she's taking it back, teasing them . . . and . . . Ehmagawd, she's making them cross their hearts and hope to die. . . . Now she's . . . Ew! She's giving them each a . . . *Ewwwwww!*"

"Ewwwwww!" everyone screamed.

"Did she just kiss my brother?" Claire shouted over the screech of Porsche tires and scream of angry guitars.

"And Tiny Nathan!" Alicia squealed as the bright yellow car zipped off down the street.

Relief warmed Massie's icy fingertips like a pair of Chanel lambskin-and-fox-fur gloves. The beautiful blonde who hung out with high school guys and who had created the fashion trend Massie secretly labeled "dancey couture" wasn't at the Block estate to buy something of Claire's. She hadn't lost her cool and become an FOC. Skye Hamilton was as alpha as ever. An anxious flutter wormed its way through Massie's belly.

So why *was* she there?

Digging her thumb into the white remote, she shouted, before the window had fully opened, "Bring that envelope up here ay-sap!"

Todd and Tiny Nathan were too busy running around the wagon, giggling and punching each other, to respond.

"Todd, I mean it!" Massie shouted.

"Todddd!" Claire echoed.

Massie tugged the gold crown on her charm bracelet, desperate to know what was inside that envelope. And more important, whom it was for.

"Want me to sit on his chest and fart?" Dylan asked with a hopeful smile. "Kristen can tackle him and I can—"

"Not necessary." Massie held her palm in front of Dylan's emerald green eyes. "I got this." She winked, then cupped her hands around her mouth and yelled, "Alicia, put your shirt back on!"

Todd and Tiny Nathan froze.

Alicia gasped. Massie quickly gave her a play-along-or-change-schools look.

The boys' shoulders were shaking with laughter as they buried their faces in their gray Gap hoodies.

"Let's *all* take our shirts off," Dylan bellowed.

"I'm in!" Kristen grabbed the brown Ella Moss T-shirt dress off Massie's floor and tossed it out the window. "Wow, I feel so free!"

"Me too!" Dylan lobbed a white Petit Bateaux tank.

Massie reached into the pile of clothes beside her mannequin, grabbed a handful of skinny jeans, and whipped them into the cool April breeze.

Moments later, the Blocks' lawn was covered in rejected back-to-school clothes, and Todd and Tiny Nathan stood panting in Massie's doorway, wearing matching army green Crocs and clutching a reflective gold envelope.

"I told you they were faking." Tiny Nathan punched the inside of the empty red money belt strapped to his narrow hips.

Massie lunged toward Todd and plucked the pristine envelope from his sweaty grip. Everyone rushed to her side.

Bean crawled under the oatmeal-colored cashmere blanket on her princess doggie bed and sighed.

"No, I told *you*." Todd smacked his petite friend on the back of the arm. His money belt jingled like a Unicef box on Halloween.

"No, I told *you*!"

"It's not addressed to *anyone*!" Kristen blurted.

"What did Skye say when she gave it to you?" Claire asked her brother. Before he could answer, Massie ripped open the sticky seal and dumped the contents on her purple duvet.

"A CD?" Dylan asked.

"Is it labeled?" Kristen leaned closer.

Massie read the miniature gold letters on the spine. "It says ALPHA."

"That's us!" Alicia bounced in her yellow patent leather ballet flats.

Massie hurried to her G5 and fed it the mysterious disc. She had a hunch about the contents but didn't want to say anything. Not until she was sure. Her heart thumped while she waited for the computer to stop wheezing like an asthmatic and read the CD.

Alicia's chocolaty Angel perfume, mixed with Claire's sugary gummy-worm breath, mixed with Kristen's coconut-scented Paul Mitchell mousse, mixed with Dylan's watermelon Bubble Yum, mixed with Todd and Tiny Nathan's corn-soaked Frito fingers, engulfed her.

"Everyone take five steps back!"

Massie waited for the sound of retreating footsteps on her hardwood floors. "If your name is Todd or Tiny Nathan, you have three minutes to gather my clothes from the lawn and deposit them in the laundry room. If you don't, I will tell everyone at OCD and Briarwood Academy that you peed your pants when Skye Hamilton kissed you. One Miss Sixty . . . two Miss Sixty . . . three Miss Sixty . . . four—"

Thanks to the reflection on her twenty-inch computer screen, Massie didn't have to turn around to see the 10-year-old boys shoving each other out her bedroom door.

Suddenly, the *ffhhht* sound of a match striking a scratch pad came through her speakers. Then a *whoosh*. A smooth, pale female hand illuminated by an orange flame came into focus. It was lighting the wick of a white Tocca votive.

Everyone gasped. Massie wiped her clammy hands over the purple faux-fur padding on her desk chair.

"Ehmagawd, that's Skye's mouth," Kristen pointed to the Ferrari-red lips that filled the screen. "I can tell by that little beauty mark to the right of her philtrum."

"Her *what*?" Massie hit pause.

"The philtrum is that groove between the nose and the lips," Kristen announced. "Sorry, I assumed everyone knew that."

"Maybe everyone named Wikipedia," Dylan snapped.

"Quiet." Massie pressed play.

The camera pulled back, revealing a close-up of Skye's flawless face. Her thick, buttery blond waves and Tiffany-box blue eyes, along with the warm flicker of the candle, made looking at her head-on painful, like staring straight into a beautiful sunset.

"If you are watching this," Skye whispered, her raspy voice crackling like cellophane wrap on a gift basket, *"you have been chosen."*

"Ehmagawd!" Massie hit pause again and swiveled her chair around. "I knew it. She's giving me the key!"

"So the key is really real?" Alicia squealed.

"What key?" Claire asked.

"Does this mean the *room* is really real?" Kristen crinkled her eyebrows.

"*What* room?"

"So is key season legit?" Dylan spit her gum into Massie's mosaic-tiled trash can.

"What is *key season*?" Claire stomped her watermelon-spotted Keds.

"Allow me," Alicia insisted. She gathered her shiny black hair into a smart bun and fastened it with a silver Tiffany pen from Massie's desk. "Rumor has it there's a secret room at OCD the teachers forgot about, and the alpha eighth grader has the key—"

"It's not a rumor, it's true," Dylan interrupted.

"It's a rumor until it's proven true," Kristen insisted. "Alicia, have you ever *seen* it?"

"Opposite of yes."

"Then it's a rumor."

"It's true!" Massie tapped her freshly manicured nails on her keyboard. "I can feel it. Ehmagawd! We are so set for eighth grade." She hit play.

"What you are about to see is classified," Skye continued, her expression serious and grave. *"If you can't keep a secret, please eject this CD-ROM and destroy it. Failure to keep the following information confidential will result in the DSL Daters ejecting and destroying you."* An offscreen chorus whisper-chanted, *"Eject . . . eject . . . eject . . . destroy . . . destroy . . . destroy,"* while Skye stared at Massie.

"This is freaking me out." Alicia folded her arms across her chest.

"Same," Dylan echoed.

"If this is still playing, you have agreed to carry the secret of the key for the rest of your life—the key that unlocks the door to paradise."

All of a sudden, the chorus from Nelly's song "Paradise" blasted through Massie's speakers.

Paradise
That's what she said to me
Paradise

Glittery animated images of rainbows and suns and stars pulsed on to the screen to the soulful beat of the music. Then they stopped, and Skye returned.

"This five-year tradition began when a certain major loser of an eighth-grader found the key to an abandoned room on campus. . . ."

A picture of a tall, gawky LBR standing in front of her locker with a pink knockoff pashmina draped over a barf-yellow boiled wool turtleneck appeared on the screen. Her face was covered with a clip-art picture of a gold key to conceal her identity.

"She snuck in with her friends, turned it into a secret hang spot, and invited a few Briarwood boys over during lunch. Within a week, these girls were the new alphas. And the old alphas were done—"

Massie hit pause.

Without saying a single word, she stared at Skye's frozen face on the screen and imagined what it must have been like to be the alpha who got usurped by a pack of knockoff-pashmina-wearing LBRs. The thought made her stomach churn and her scalp tighten. It was the closest thing to physical pain she had ever known.

"Um, hu-llo?" Alicia waved a hand in front of Massie's eyes.

"Sorry." She fluffed her hair and pressed play.

"When she went to high school, she passed the key on to the coolest girl she knew, who happened to be a true alpha. So from that moment on, the key always went to the OCD elite. And now I'm doing the same."

"Yes! She knows I'm the coolest." Massie gripped the computer screen and kissed it, leaving a shiny Crème Brûlée–flavored Glossip Girl lip print in the center. "The Pretty Committee will finally have a private place to hold meetings! I am so hiring a decorator over the summer."

"Let's load it with animal-print furniture from the Ralph Lauren Home collection." Alicia beamed. "The new line is insane!"

"Done." Massie cranked up the volume, not wanting to miss a single syllable.

"Take a look at some of the things we did."

One by one, photographs of "the room"—which was half the size of a classroom, and windowless—faded onto the screen. There was a shot of three girls lying on pink beach towels surrounded by white sand and matching bikinis, their faces hidden by animated smiley emoticons. A giant sun-lamp beamed down on them.

"Is that sand *inside* the room?" Claire asked. "It looks like they're at the beach."

"Shhhhhh," the girls snapped.

The next shot showed them leaning against a juice bar made of palm fronds and leaves. It reminded Massie of the Sugar Shack, a poolside smoothie hut she'd frequented during her family's vacation in Tonga.

"Is that juice bar *inside* the room?"

"Shhhhh!"

The third shot showed four grinning emoticons with their eyes closed in cushy black recliners getting pedicures from four shirtless high school guys. Rose petals covered the floors, and HAPPY VALENTINE'S DAY was spelled out on the wall behind them in red-foil-covered Hershey's Kisses.

"Ehmagawd." Kristen rubbed her flat abs. "I'll have a place to hide the clothes my mom won't let me wear. I won't have to change in the Range Rover anymore!"

"Let's hire that goth barista to work in there." Dylan beamed. "We'll buy a Starbucks machine, make her wear a green apron, and teach her how to make those enormous fat-free blueberry muffins. We'll text our orders and zip over between classes to pick them up."

"Can we dig a tunnel that leads to Briarwood so the boys can sneak in?" Claire asked.

"Love it all!" Massie tapped all their suggestions into her PalmPilot. "Done, done, and done."

The photos faded away, and candlelit Skye returned. *"And there's something else in the room that's way too incredible for your little seventh-grade eyes to see."* Skye winked at the camera. *"But it will be yours . . . if you are the first one to find the key."*

Massie smacked pause.

"First one to find it? Who else will be looking for it?" She ran a shaky hand through her chestnut brown layers. "Don't I automatically get it?"

"Yeah," huffed Alicia. "I thought it got handed down from one alpha to the next."

"It's probably just a formality," Kristen suggested. "Like how you have to say the name of your favorite radio station before you win the concert tickets."

Massie took a deep breath to calm her quaking hands, then pressed play.

"Since it's the fifth anniversary of the room, I'm going to break tradition and do something different. Instead of automatically handing the key off to the seventh-grade alpha, I'm turning this into a contest and have sent out five CD-ROMs to a wide range of girls. This way, nonalphas have the chance to become alphas, just as our great founders did, five years ago. And I've hidden the key under the mattress of a highly respectable Westchester boy who understands that being an alpha is about more than having the right clothes—"

"Yes!" Kristen punched the air.

"It's about staying true to yourself, no matter what anyone else thinks."

Dylan stuffed a piece of bubble gum in her mouth and slurped back the onslaught of watermelon-flavored spit.

"I hereby dedicate the key, and the following poem, to him." Skye's Tiffany box–colored eyes glistened with tears. Massie couldn't help wondering if the effect had been added in Photoshop.

Biting her lip, Skye closed her eyes and began. Her words floated across the screen in a pink glittery script that

seemed too cute and playful for the low, raspy voice reciting
them.

> The boy who sleeps atop the key
> Is into the exact same things as me.
> He loves all creatures, big and small,
> So his age doesn't matter, not at all.
> I try not to think about his "Glamour-don't" style
> By focusing on his kick-butt smile.
> Note to self: I've kissed this guy,
> But I've kissed them all. How bad am I?
> We already rode off into the sunset together,
> But the next time we do, it will be forever.
> Holla!

The pink glittery script faded away and Skye's lips
returned.

*"Talking about this to anyone, including me or the DSL
Daters, is against the rules. Searching for the room before you
are in possession of the key is against the rules. And asking
any boy if I have been to his house is a waste of time. The
answer will always be yes. If you find the key, wear the Coach
key chain with the little handbags on it around your neck. Then
wait. I will contact you. May the true alpha win."* Skye blew
out the Tocca votive candle. A swirling gray ribbon of smoke
twisted in the darkness, eventually giving up and fading. The
screen was black.

"May the best alpha win?" Massie whacked her computer. "How many alphas does she think there *are* in the seventh grade?"

The image of Carrie Randolph and her BFFs Alexandra Regan (metal mouth) and Livvy Collins (lip-gloss eater) ruling the room popped into her head. The make-out virgins would probably throw parent-supervised girls-only parties where they'd talk about the latest technology in braces and the best-tasting balms. All this while the Pretty Committee roamed the cold, bustling halls in last year's calf-high Kors boots, searching for a warm place to hang.

"What if someone else wins?" Dylan anxiously tore a subscription card out of Alicia's *Teen Vogue*, then folded it around her chewed gum.

"Im-possible." Alicia batted the air. "This is our destiny."

"It better be," Massie brooded, a massive to-do list forming in her head.

"Shhhh." Kristen lifted a finger to her lips. "We're not allowed to talk about this with anyone."

"Point."

"That can't possibly apply to *us*," Massie whispered, just in case.

"Point."

Massie turned her back on the naked mannequin and snapped into drill-sergeant mode. "Kristen, put a file together of Skye's hobbies. Alicia, I need names of the boys she's kissed. Dylan, find out who else got this CD-ROM. And

Claire, ask Todd what she said to him. We'll go over everything tomorrow during lunch."

"What's *your* job?" Claire asked, sounding genuinely curious.

"My job?" Massie faced her army and lifted her chin.
"My job is to win."

Claire gazed at the Hogwarts-esque stone building, with its elegant turrets and landscaped grounds, then zipped her powder blue down jacket all the way to the very top. As she often had before, she found herself wondering how the rest of the Pretty Committee could manage to go jacketless on such a gray, blustery day. Granted, they were about to make their grand reentrance to OCD and didn't want their well-crafted outfits marred by coats and scarves and gloves. But didn't they feel the angry wind winding its way through the spaces between their bones? Or the finger-numbing chill of winter? Did they not feel *cold*?

It was the first time Isaac, the Blocks' driver, had dropped them off in the rear parking lot, and the first time Claire had seen her school from that angle. The back was as majestic as the front, yet something about the view made her feel lonely.

"Ew." Alicia winced, scanning the rows of fuel-efficient Fords and Toyotas. "These cars are so Toys 'R' Us. Why are we *here*? Can't we go around front where the normal people park?"

"No," Massie huffed, in an I'm-only-going-to-explain-this-one-last-time sort of way. "We need a private place for final outfit inspections. Besides, you may want to spend a minute or two on your hair. The wind has not been kind."

"Why? What's wrong with it?" Alicia scurried to the side mirror of a white Volkswagen Jetta and finger-combed her highly envied black shoulder-length waves.

"Kuh-laire, doesn't Judi have one of *those*?" Dylan pointed to the bronze-colored Taurus sandwiched between a blue Corolla and a yellow Camry.

Claire's stomach lurched. "It's just a *rental*," she snapped, instantly hating herself for feeling embarrassed by her mother's affordable car. But the last thing she wanted on her first day back was to be any more self-conscious than she already was.

Usually, this anxious niggling struck Claire the night before she entered a new grade. Or after a long Christmas break away from her friends. But never in April. And *never* this hard. It was a frustrating blend of excitement and fear, the kind that made her want to run and freeze at the same time.

Claire flipped the red cap on the bottle of Evian she'd taken from the mini-fridge in the Blocks' Range Rover and chugged, hoping to drown what felt like thousands of fuzzy caterpillars squirming behind her belly button.

On one hand, she couldn't wait to get back to the warm familiarity of old classrooms and classmates. But on the other, she was afraid. No, she was terrified. Terrified that starring in *Dial L for Loser* would make her stand out, when all she'd ever wanted was to fit in.

"Is anyone else kind of freaked right now?" An air cloud puffed from Kristen's heart-shaped mouth. "You know, like nervous?"

Claire nodded in her mind.

"Nervous?" Alicia asked Massie, like she was checking to see if that emotion had been approved. But Massie was far too busy dabbing her wrists with Chanel No. 5 to tell anyone how to feel. That, or she was battling first-day jitters of her own.

"Yeah, you know, cuz we've been gone for so long and everything." Kristen pinched her cheeks pink. "What if we can't catch up on our homework?"

"That's what you're worried about?" Dylan spit a wad of green gum onto the cold pavement. *"Homework?"*

"Yeah." Kristen blushed. "Why? What are *you* worried about?"

Massie rolled her eyes and then, without warning, began making her way across the parking lot.

Everyone followed.

"Nothing," Dylan whisper-snapped defensively. "But if I *was*, I'd be worried everyone forgot about us and that they won't notice we're back." She swung her striped denim Fendi Spy bag back and forth. "Not that I *am* worried about that. Because I'm *nawt.*"

"Ehmagawd, do you think anyone's been sitting at table eighteen for lunch?" Alicia asked as she tiptoed across the freshly mowed lawn, probably to keep the dew off her brown suede boots. "What if they don't give it back?"

Massie choke-coughed twice, and then sped up. She didn't utter a single word until they crossed the field and reached the deserted side door entrance. Silently, she directed them to line up against the uneven stone building.

"Wardrobe check!" She beamed, the fun finally returning to her amber eyes.

Everyone rolled their shoulders and puffed out their chests, except Claire. Instead, she buried her chin in the puffy collar of her coat and prayed for invisibility.

"Alicia, let's start with you."

"Yayyy." She hugged herself, stepped forward, and then twirled.

Massie held an imaginary microphone in front of her mouth, then began. "Alicia is looking lovely in a denim, vintage-inspired, shrunken Polo blazer with a navy silk tank and a faded Hudson jean skirt over navy stretch pants. A chocolate-brown belt and matching suede ankle boots complete the look. Her hair, which was ahb-viously blown dry with a diffuser, is looking full and extra bouncy. Congratulations: you are a nine point five."

Everyone golf-clapped while Alicia curtsied.

"Dylan?" Massie signaled the redhead to step forward.

"Here." She burped, and then twirled the way Todd would if he were imitating a ballerina.

"As usual, you look comfy-cool in a black Ella Moss tie-back sleeveless jumpsuit with gold cowboy boots and a thick gold waist belt. Your hair has been straightened and deep-conditioned to perfection. But something is missing. . . .

Hmmm . . ." She tapped her lower lip. "I know! A touch of rosy blush."

"Done." Dylan reached into her denim makeup case and pulled out a gold YSL compact.

"Congratulations: you are a nine point three."

Dylan bowed while the girls giggle-clapped with pride.

Much to Claire's relief, Kristen automatically stepped forward and spun, her arms splayed out to the side.

"Looking sporty-chic in a blousy orange-and-white-striped rugby tee and black short shorts is Kristen Gregory. She gets extra points for ditching that mom-approved, floor-length peasant skirt in the back of my Range Rover. And extra, extra points for the ah-dorable side braid. Congratulations, you are a nine point four."

Kristen high-fived Alicia and Dylan.

Claire, knowing she was nowhere near a nine, examined the silver zipper on her jacket pocket, hoping Massie would forget about her, just this once.

"Kuh-laire?"

"Yeah." She lifted her eyes.

"Are you a zit?"

"No."

"Then why are you all covered up?"

Everyone giggled.

"I'm cold." She bounced on the toes of her denim Keds for effect. "You can skip over me."

"That would mean an automatic two," Massie warned.

The girls gasped.

"S'okay," Claire assured her, preferring the low rating to a round of Old Navy jokes.

"You know that anything lower than a seven means you have to walk three paces behind us all day," Alicia was quick to add.

She didn't.

"You may wanna change your mind," Kristen urged.

Claire started weighing the pros and cons. Walking beside them on the first day back would definitely take some of the edge off. But what if they laughed at her pink-and-purple floral waffle shirt? Would she even *want* to walk beside them? Or would she run to the nearest bathroom, sob, and spend the rest of the day wishing she'd worn the stylish but itchy maroon V-necked sweater dress Massie had lent her?

"Too late!" Dylan tapped her green quartz ToyWatch.

"But—"

Massie held out her palm until Claire closed her mouth. Then she stepped and twirled. "I'm wearing a gray Geren Ford V-necked kimono dress with a super-chunky black suede belt that hangs diagonally across my hips. A pair of black leggings are peeking out the bottom, while red patent leather flats add a burst of color at my ankles. My hair is in a low side chignon and fastened with two red chopsticks." She placed her hands on her hips and grinned. "Feedback?"

"Nine point six," Alicia offered immediately.

"Ah-greed," Dylan and Kristen confirmed.

Claire nodded.

"What would make me a nine point *eight*?" Massie spun again while the girls studied her.

"A touch more gloss," Alicia blurted with total certainty.

"Ah-greed," echoed the others.

"Okay." Massie coated her lips with Rice Krispy Treat Glossip Girl. "On the count of three, everyone sing the chorus of 'Don't Cha' by the Pussycat Dolls in your head. That way we'll all be walking to the same beat. Oh, Kuh-laire, you should start three seconds later, since you'll be behind us."

"But—"

"Ready?" Massie wrapped her hand around the silver pump handle on the lacquered wood door and mouthed, *"One . . . two . . . three . . . Don't cha wish your girlfriend was hot like me?"* Once the others were whisper-singing along, she pushed the handle and burst into the hall, Alicia on her right, Dylan and Kristen on her left.

Claire inhaled deeply, fighting the pinch behind her eyes, as she watched her friends take off without her. Maybe Hollywood was the right place for her after all.

After counting to three, she entered the building to the sultry beat in her head. *"Don't cha wish your girlfriend was hot like me? Don't cha wish your girlfriend was a freak like me?"*

Once inside, the scent of bitter coffee and Xerox chemicals ambushed Claire, making her momentarily lose her place in the song. She'd forgotten how different the hall smelled on the teachers' side and relished the familiarity of it all.

With every synchronized step Claire took, the louder the pre-morning bell sounds became; overlapping conversations, explosions of laughter, boot heels squeaking, slamming metal locker doors. The moment of truth was upon them.

Massie lifted her bronzed arm in the air and snapped twice.

It was time.

They made a sharp right and merged flawlessly with the heavy flow of student traffic.

A mix of flowery perfume, fruity hair products, and sweet bubble gum replaced the stale church smell that hovered around the teachers' section. The water fountains seemed lower and the halls narrower than Claire remembered. But other than that, girls were whizzing and whirling in a mad rush to make it to class on time, just like they always had. Claire took in the scene and sigh-smiled. Everything was more or less exactly how she'd left it.

"You guys! They're back!" shouted Allie-Rose Singer, who towered a good foot over every other girl in the seventh grade. The black-haired green-eyed beauty was far too tall to be in the Pretty Committee, according to Massie, which was a shame, since her wardrobe was filled with all of the desirables—cashmere cowl-neck sweaters, dark skinny jeans, silk tunics, sweater dresses, and shiny Marc Jacobs flats in every color. But everything was too long to share, rendering Allie-Rose and her fabulous wardrobe useless.

"Welcome!" She dropped the stack of textbooks she had

been clutching, smoothed her navy button-down shirtdress, and clapped.

All of a sudden, everyone in the halls noticed them and joined in the applause.

Like a school of colorful sunfish, the Pretty Committee stopped at the exact same time. Claire, who was still walking to "Don't Cha," stepped on the back of Massie's red leather flat, causing her heel to slip out. She felt her cheeks flush in anticipation of the stretch-limo-size verbal slap she would undoubtedly get. But like a true professional, Massie slipped her foot back inside without so much as a wobble while waving to her devoted public with the grace of a prom queen.

Technically, starting the day greeted by hordes of stylish, adoring fans was a good thing. But for some reason, Claire found the attention overwhelming. What was she supposed to do with her hands? Let them dangle at her sides? Wave? Applaud *them* for applauding *her*? And what about her expression? Should she appear shocked and humbled? Or deserving and proud? The only thing Claire knew for sure was that all of this hooting and hollering made her cheeks burn and her head all light and tingly. Her face felt like a giant red helium balloon and her body a flimsy string.

All she could do was take advantage of her position in the back row and take cover behind the girls.

"Ta-da!" Allie-Rose yanked a string above her head. Dozens of purple balloons fell from a net above her locker.

"Ehmagawd, purple's my favorite color," Massie gushed, like it was some sort of coincidence.

"We know," beamed Penelope Rothman, whose dimples dented her freckled cheeks like giant fingernail marks. She pointed to the purple-glitter-soaked "GR8 2 C U" banners with the grace of a seasoned flight attendant.

"Ooooh," squealed Alicia, once she saw the life-size cardboard cutouts of her and Massie, taken straight from the glossy pages of *Us Weekly*. "I heart *those*!"

Pictures of them swimming with Conner Foley in his Malibu Beach pool were plastered on the outside of the girls' lockers alongside blown-up shots of Dylan and her talk-show-host mother Merri-Lee Marvil, taken from an old article from *Vanity Fair* about celebrities and their daughters.

"Hurry, before the bell rings," announced Paige Winman, who managed to get away with her too-short-even-for-a-boy cut because she was the best abstract painter at OCD. She was leading a swarm of girls armed with Sharpie minis and cell-phone cameras. She forced her way between Dylan and Kristen, red-rover style, waving a color copy of the not-yet-released *Dial L for Loser* movie poster. "Claire will you *please* sign this? I've had it pressed in my atlas for days, waiting for you to get back."

Claire giggled when she saw her flawless, airbrushed face. She was posed on a lunch table, legs crossed, in a crowded cafeteria, wearing a skimpy private school uniform and holding a crystal-covered cell phone to her ear, winking in a shhh-don't-tell sort of way. In the background, Conner Foley was kissing Abby Boyd but looking at Claire, longingly. It was perfect.

"How did you get this?"

"I found it on the Internet and made copies," she boasted.

"We all have one," said Erica Lunsky, gesturing to the snaking line of starstruck girls forming behind her. "Will you sign them before class?"

Claire didn't want to let her fans down, but she also knew not to be late on her first day back. "Um, sure." She checked her pink Baby G-Shock watch. "If we hurry."

One by one, Claire worked her way through the line, each time signing her name a little differently. She signed Kami Kauffman's like this:

Claire Lyons

and Dara Sammet's like this:

Claire Lyons

and Payton Lawrie's like this:

CLAIRE
Y
O
N
S

until, finally, she came up with what was sure to be an eBay-worthy autograph:

The five-minute warning bell rang and Claire's heart quickened. She hadn't even taken off her jacket yet, let alone fumbled with her lock and fished out her American history book. Beads of light sweat gathered on her forehead as she forced her hand to sign faster. But the faster she signed, the more she sweated. And the more she sweated, the stringier her bangs became.

"Will you call my older sister and tell her you know me?" asked Olivia Ryan, Alicia's beautiful ex-BFF. A glittery black-and-gold beret was angled atop her blond curls, giving a Parisian spin to her otherwise standard-issue skinny black jeans and simple white Oxford.

"Uh, can I do it after class?"

"Call my sister, too," Candace Sheppard begged.

"You don't have a sister." Olivia shoved her orange Nokia in Claire's face, accidentally bashing her nose.

"Ouch!" Claire doubled over.

"Can I take your picture?" asked Emily Kohn, holding a lime green Motorola Pebl directly between Claire's eyes.

"Uh . . ." Claire glanced at Massie, desperate to be saved. But she, Alicia, and Dylan were too busy signing magazine photos, pencil cases, and backpacks to notice. Kristen was the only one free to go to her locker. And while her slow shuffle and dejected pout indicated that she wasn't happy about her lack of attention, Claire found herself almost envying it.

The final bell rang.

"Let's pick this up at lunch," Massie called to her groupies. "Table eighteen."

A hurried round of thank-you-sooooo-muches and welcome-backs were fired at the Pretty Committee as everyone scattered.

"Hollywood was fun, but I like Westchester better." Alicia fumbled with her lock. "We're way more famous here."

"Whatevs." Kristen slammed her locker. "I hope you feel *famous* getting a late pass," she shouted, and then hurried to class.

"Oh, we will!" Dylan called after her.

"What's *her* problem?" Alicia asked on their way to Principal Burns's office.

"Not enough FOKs" Massie shrugged in a sucks-for-her sort of way.

"Huh?"

"Fans of Kristen."

Dylan giggled.

"I double-dog heart that," Alicia squealed.

Claire sat between Dylan and Alicia on the hard wooden bench outside the principal's door, thinking about the secret pro/con list she had tucked away in her jacket pocket.

2 MOVE OR NOT 2 MOVE?

CALIFORNI-YAY	CALIFORNI-NAY
Photography is my favorite hobby. ☺ But acting is my second. ☺☺ And I'll get to star in movies and play the kind of girls everyone wants to be. ☺☺☺ BONUS: If I ever come back, I'll automatically get the lead in the school play (unless it's a musical). ☺	Leaving Cam. ☹ Again. ☹ ☹
I will possibly meet and have sleepovers with Dakota Fanning. ☺☺☺☺☺☺☺☺☺☺☺☺	Leaving the Pretty Committee and Layne. ☹
I'll make millions of dollars. Maybe enough to buy my mom a silver Porsche convertible. ☺☺☺☺	Moving to a new city again. ☹ Starting over again. ☹☹☹☹☹ ☹☹☹☹☹☹☹☹☹☹☹☹☹
I will have a stylist who will make me look like a 9.8 every day. ☺☺☺	I have fans in Westchester. Possibly more than Massie???? (Not that I would ever say that to her.)
No more puffy jackets. ☺☺ Warm weather, palm trees, beaches, and flip-flops all year round. ☺☺☺☺☺☺	The fall is kind of nice. I like when the leaves change colors. I will miss that. ☹

"Send in the delinquents," squawked a familiar old lady's voice from behind the beveled glass door. "One. At. A. Time."

At that moment, if someone had asked Claire which she would prefer: (a) to be a nonfamous nobody again or (b) to get mobbed by tons of fans and then have to ask Principal

Burns for a late slip, she would have picked (a) in a second.

The revelation shocked her. She used to lie awake at night making arrangements with God, like that if he made the girls at OCD like her, she'd fold her clothes the way her mother asked instead of stuffing them behind her armoire. But now that Claire was front-page news, she surprised herself by wanting out of this divine deal and made a mental note to delete "I have fans in Westchester" from her 2 Move or Not 2 Move list. It was creepy watching people buy her clothes and boring spending her Sunday choosing crowd-pleasing outfits. She didn't want to strut to the beat of a slutty song. She didn't want to worry how her sweaty bangs might look in cell-phone pictures. And she *really* didn't want to be late for class.

"Ms. Block!" Principal Burns shouted. "Enter!"

Flashing her friends a she-so-doesn't-scare-me eye-roll, Massie rose. "Did you see how many people wanted our autographs?" she leaned in and whispered, like that somehow made it all worth it. "I think I saw a few eighth graders there too. Hopefully they'll tell Skye we—"

"Now!"

Snickering, Massie raced toward the principal's office, gently closing the door behind her.

Claire sat on her shaking hands, wondering how Massie handled it all—the attention, the pressure, the jacketless winters. . . . Or maybe the better question was, why did she *want* to?

The lunch crowd rubbernecked as they passed the Pretty Committee's prestigious windowside table—which thankfully had been roped off with purple ribbon, thanks to Allie-Rose's connection in the art department—hoping for a glimpse at OCD's first real-life celebrities.

"Hey, Claire," Kaya Horner gushed as she strolled by, swinging an empty red tray. The petite, tights-obsessed brunette was dressed in a black cashmere turtleneck and a faded pair of tattered cut-off Sevens, which she wore over white-and-gray-striped Hues. Her legs looked like two gangly Slinkys. "I cannot *wait* to see your moo-vie."

Lowering her spaghetti-covered fork for the third time that minute, Claire smiled and kindly said, "Awww, thanks."

Massie rolled her eyes. "Gawd, can we puh-lease talk about you-know-what"—she mimed turning a key in a door—"without getting interrupted by LBR FOCs?"

"Welcome back, Massie," waved Mindy Baum, head of the student council. As usual, she was wearing an extra-small OCD STUDENT BODY baby tee, this one in hot pink. "We missed you guys."

"Thanks." Massie cupped her chignon. "We ah-dore the colorful confetti on our table. That had to be you guys, right?"

"Totally." Mindy blushed.

Dylan nestled her head in the C-shaped pillow that had been tied to the back of her orange plastic cafeteria chair. "Did you make these too?"

"I can't take all the credit." Mindy motioned for five DIY-loving girls at table 14 to stand. "We had a little help from the Crafts Club."

They climbed up on their chairs and bowed, each girl wearing the club's signature paisley smock over ultra-flared jeans and a vintage-inspired blouse.

"Thread-heads," Massie murmured as she applauded their efforts with what looked, to the untrained eye, like absolute sincerity. Then she waved goodbye to Mindy, letting her know in no uncertain terms that it was time for her to leave.

"I heart the flowers the Shakespeare Club stuck in our poetry books." Alicia caressed the white rose behind her ear. "They're so ah-dork-able."

"I know." Massie giggled. "Sweet in a sad way."

"Clairenoticeanythingfamiliar?" interrupted Carrie Randolph while tugging at the pink-and-red polka-dot scarf around her neck.

"Oh, wow!" Claire feigned excitement. "You bought that from Todd, right?"

"Itcostmethreeweeksallowencebutitwastotallyworthit."

"Fast talker!" Dylan sneezed.

Everyone laughed, but Carrie didn't seem to notice.

"Umwhendoes*DialLforLoser*comeoutcauseIamtotally wearingthistothetheater."

"Memorial Day weeke—"

"Great, Cathy, thanks so much for the visit." Massie clapped twice.

"It's Ca-rrie," she huffed.

Massie double-clapped again.

Carrie turned and stormed off.

Massie crumpled her white paper napkin and tossed it on her uneaten California rolls. "We *totally* need a private room."

You didn't have to be so mean, Claire felt like saying. But secretly she was relieved Carrie was gone. Accepting all of this attention and praise over a movie no one had seen felt dishonest, like getting an A on a test she hadn't taken.

Massie leaned forward. One second later, the Pretty Committee was nose-to-nose in the center of the table. "So. In the poem? When Skye was talking about *Glamour*-don't style? Who do you think she meant?"

"Derrington," Kristen offered, with a trace of leftover nobody-wanted-my-autograph jealousy.

"He *does* wear shorts in the winter." Dylan bit into her turkey-bacon burger with low-fat cheddar.

"Point."

"According to the poem, that means she *kissed* him." Massie bit her lower lip.

Claire wanted to ask how Skye and Derrington knew each other and if anyone thought they had been "knowing each other" behind Massie's back. But she didn't, for obvious reasons.

"Do you think he cheated on me?"

Claire tugged an errant cuticle, Dylan picked a sesame seed off her bun, Alicia checked for split ends, and Kristen folded her napkin into a tiny, tiny rectangle.

"Ehmagawd!" Massie managed, despite the thumping heart in her throat. "You think he *cheated* on me?"

Kristen opened her mouth.

"Ehmagawd, you do!"

"No, I—"

"Stand up, you!" bellowed Kori Gedman as she approached their table. A tight tan sweater accentuated her notoriously bad posture. She looked like a croissant. "I have to see what you're wearing. Everyone in third period was raving."

Her best friend, Strawberry, was beside her, dressed in a dark pink off-the-shoulder sweatshirt that matched her berry-colored hair. "Yeah, let's see."

Massie, Alicia, Dylan, and Kristen pushed back their chairs. A symphony of screeching metal sliced through the buzzing lunchtime chatter, causing a roomful of heads to turn their way.

One at a time, each girl gave her best supermodel spin.

"No, I want to see *Claire*." Kori's arched neck shot forward.

Claire's cheeks felt hotter than the Blocks' Jacuzzi.

"Yeah," nodded Strawberry. "We want to see what a real movie star wears."

"Ha!" Massie blurted, then quickly covered her mouth, like it had just slipped out.

"Come on." Kori shook her tray of Tater Tots. "Show us."

Lifting her light blond eyebrows apologetically, Claire tried to remind Massie that she hadn't asked for any of this.

Massie fired back a yeah-right glare.

Ignoring the jealous whispers of her supposed BFFs, Claire stood.

"Cute top." Kori bit her thumbnail while she scanned Claire's pink-and-purple-flowered thermal. "Is it a Marc Jacobs?"

"No," Alicia answered for her. "It's a Marc *Down*."

Giggles erupted from the Pretty Committee.

Claire sat.

"How much do you love her?" Kori cooed to no one in particular. "She's still so down-to-earth."

"Look." Strawberry wiggled her foot. "I'm wearing Keds. You totally got me into them."

"Same." Kori revealed the light blue slip-ons from the Rave line, the same ones Claire had worn on the movie set. They must have seen them in the interviews. "Which ones do you have on?"

Claire poked her leg out from under the table. "Denim Champion Destroyed."

"Love those!"

"Know what KEDS stands for?" Massie interrupted.

Kori and Strawberry shook their heads.

"It means Kuh-laire, E-nuf Discussing Shoes!"

Claire tried to laugh with everyone else.

"Can I just ask one thing about your jeans? Is that a

light wash or are they naturally faded?" Kori tucked a chunk of butterscotch-colored hair behind one elfin ear.

"Enough!" Massie slammed her hands on the table. A geyser of pastel confetti shot into the air. "We're in the middle of something, okay?"

Kori and Strawberry inched back.

"She's right." Claire smiled sympathetically. "Let's catch up after school."

Strawberry's cheeks reddened with rage. She grabbed her friend's arm, pulling her away, but Kori turned and called, "Kristen, see you at soccer practice!"

"Can't wait." She lifted her palm.

Kori broke away from Strawberry and scurried back to high-five Kristen. "We're going all the way this season."

"How 'bout you go all the way back to the LBR table?" Massie shooed her away as though she were one of Dylan's salami burps. "Ugh! I can't take the constant drive-bys." She flicked a yellow piece of confetti off her gray kimono dress. "It's so ah-nnoy—"

"Welcome back!" Layne Abeley waved. Her index finger was stained bright orange.

Claire willed her friend not to stop at table eighteen, but Layne was not one to take a hint, telepathic or otherwise. She dragged a chair from a nearby table, squeezed in between Claire and Kristen, then pulled a bag of Crystal Light On the Go out of her hay-colored World Famous backpack.

"What are you *wearing*?" Claire asked, unable to hide her shock and embarrassment.

Layne's suspenders, hiking boots, and red fedora—complete with a built-in water dispenser that reached from the brim to her mouth—were farther from the pages of *Teen Vogue* than a size-eight model.

"Is *The Sound of Music* cool again?" Dylan asked.

Layne poked her finger into the bag of peach-flavored tea mix. "Excuse me for not wanting to spend my morning walking 2.3 miles in stiletto boots and a prom dress."

"Ew, who would wear stiletto boots with a prom dress?" Alicia shook at the thought.

"You *walked* to school?" asked Claire.

"Yeah, Chris wouldn't give me a ride because he wanted to visit Tricky. It's her birthday." She popped open a gold heart-shaped locket around her neck and showed Claire a picture of her brother's black horse.

"Awwww."

"I *totally* understood, but his girlfriend, Fawn, was pissed!" She removed her finger from the bag, skillfully transferring the anthill of sugar on her finger to her mouth. Then she squeezed her eyes shut. "So tart."

"L," Massie coughed.

"B," Alicia sneezed.

"R," Dylan yawned.

Kristen cackled.

"Listen, Layne, can I call you—"

"So are you moving to Hollywood or what?"

"Um, I'm not sure. I'm meeting with my agent tomorrow." Claire chewed her thumbnail. "You know, about the whole moving thing."

"Your parents gonna let you go?"

"If I'm really serious and it's a good opportunity, they'll move with me," Claire said, ignoring the Pretty Committee's four-way eye-roll.

"What about Cam?"

The mention of his name made Claire's stomach dip. "Dunno. We're gonna wait and see what happens."

"Hey, Layne?" Massie called.

"Yeah?"

Massie slapped a napkin down on the table and slid it toward Layne. It said, in dark green eyeliner, *Pretty Committee meeting in session. No Laynes allowed.*

Layne soaked her finger with spit, stuck it inside the bag of Crystal Light, and wrote *OK*, with a chalky mixture of peach-flavored crystals and saliva.

Ignoring the chorus of *ew!*s that followed her message, Layne stood and smiled. "Claire, call me tonight after *CSI Miami*."

" 'Kay." Claire blushed.

"Finally." Massie tossed her plate of California rolls in the trash. "Let's get started." She flipped open her Motorola Razr. "Let's text. For privacy."

Claire powered on her rhinestone-encrusted, special-edition *Dial L for Loser* phone—a gift from Rupert Mann, the film's director.

Seconds later, their meeting was in session.

MASSIE: K, what r Skye's hobbies?
KRISTEN: Read her Myspace profile. Luvs mini things. mini-muffins, mini-sharpies, mini-perfume samples, mini-Chicklets . . . also luvs animals, Hershey's Kisses, glitter pens & dance.

Massie's thumbs scuttled across her keypad.

MASSIE: D, who else got the CD-ROM?
DYLAN: Duh-livia Ryan. She's already wearing a key chain around her neck. Also Layne's alt.com BFF, Heather. Saw her making a list of boys in math. Researching others.
MASSIE: A, who has she kissed?

Alicia slid four sheets of legal-size paper facedown onto the center of the table. She looked over each shoulder, then nodded, letting them know it was safe to take a look. Claire flipped hers over, and like the others, held it close to her chest while she read.

SKYE'S KISS LIST
5th Grade (Beyond ew!)	Todd Lyons
7th Grade	Derrington (☹!)

	Josh (☹!)
	Chris Plovert
	Kemp Hurley
	Doug Landsman
	Jake Shapiro
8th Grade	Grier Biggs
	Lowell Katz
	Andy Walden
	Oliver Smalls
	Ezra Rosenberg
	Cody Hill
	Geoff Michaels
	Luis Ruiz
	P.J. Jeffries
	Billy Williams
	Lee Chan
High School	Harris Fisher
	Liam Barrett
	Yuri Butterman (aka Yuri Butt-man)

After an initial scan—to make sure Cam wasn't on it—Claire took a closer look. She couldn't believe how many boys Skye had kissed. And that Derrington was one of them.

But if it bothered Massie, she didn't show it. She calmly folded her copy and placed it in her red leather Miu Miu bag and reached for her phone.

MASSIE: A, where did u get those names?

ALICIA: Can't reveal. I want 2 b a reporter. Sources r sacred.

Massie rolled her eyes.

ALICIA: Trust me. It's legit.
MASSIE: C, did Todd say anything?
CLAIRE: Swears Skye is in love with him. That's it.
MASSIE: Did you look under his mattress last night?

Claire felt her cheeks burn. How could she have forgotten?

CLAIRE: Yeah. Not there.

She pulled a thin blue Paper Mate pen out of her back pocket and wrote a big *T* on the back of her hand so she'd remember to check the minute she got home.

KRISTEN: Where should we start?

Claire typed quickly.

CLAIRE: Harris Fisher.

After spending three long weeks in Los Angeles—without Cam—Claire found herself searching for excuses to see him.

CLAIRE: I can get us in cuz he's Cam's brother.

MASSIE: 2nite?

Claire hesitated, knowing she should probably ask Cam before making plans on his behalf. But Massie was anxious to start looking for the key. And Claire was anxious to help. Getting the Pretty Committee into Harris's bedroom would stop all the Claire's-more-into-the-West-Coast-than-Westchester comments they'd been making behind her back. Plus, it would get her a school-night lip kiss from the cutest boy she'd ever known—the perfect end to a not-so-perfect day.

"Ew! What *was* that?" Alicia screeched, after accidentally grazing the back of Claire's light blue puffy jacket with her hand. "Can't we puh-lease turn on the lights? I'm scared."

"Shhhhh," Massie hissed. "No lights."

"What are we doing back here?" Dylan insisted.

"Waiting to die." Alicia sounded on the verge of tears.

Claire was relieved to know she wasn't the only one freaking out. For the last twenty minutes, she hadn't been able to shake the feeling that they were being watched. Not by Principal Burns or even Skye—more like by God or a serial killer.

The back of the chapel was creepy as it was, with the choir's black robes hanging on hooks and the row of narrow, windowless rooms used for meditation and silent prayer. But now, in the dark, with just the bluish glow from their open cell phones to guide them, it was horror-film creepy. It smelled like stale carpet and dusty old books. And all Claire could hear was Massie rattling doorknobs and knocking lightly on walls, obviously searching for the one *thing* they were forbidden to discuss.

"Kuh-laire, did you hear back from Cam yet?" Massie jiggled the last handle.

"I left three messages and still no—"

Distant footsteps distracted her.

"What was *that*?" Alicia grabbed the back of Claire's jacket.

"Sounded like ballet flats on the chapel floor," whispered Kristen.

"More like cheap Steve Maddens," Massie corrected. "Come on." She held her cell phone in front of her and hurried toward the noise. Claire was in awe of Massie's fearlessness, especially since Alicia, Dylan, Kristen, and her were clutching one another's palms, even though they were sweaty.

"Who's here?" Massie pushed through the blue velvet wings on the side of the stage like a fed-up Broadway actress and flicked on the lights.

Kaya and Penelope ducked behind a pew.

Massie glanced at Dylan and air-scribbled, letting her know to add Kaya and Penelope to the list of girls who got Skye's CD-ROM.

Dylan flashed her the thumbs-up.

"I see you."

"So?" called Kaya, still crouched like a chipmunk. "It's not a crime to be here."

"Actually, it is." Kristen put her hands on her hips. "No one is allowed to be on school property after hours unless accompanied by a member of the faculty. It says so in the OCD handbook."

"Then why are *you* here?" Penelope straightened up and

twirled her curly brown high-pony. As usual, she was dressed like a burglar, in black AG cords and a black turtleneck.

"I lost my keys," Massie jumped in.

The two girls exchanged a glance.

"In the *chapel*?" Kaya stood beside her partner in crime.

"Yeah. I was praying this morning." Massie smirked. "But it didn't work. You're still ah-nnoying."

Kaya gasped.

The Pretty Committee giggled.

"Penelope, are you a big boob?"

"No." She snorted.

"Then why are you hanging?"

The Pretty Committee burst out laughing.

"You heard her," Alicia snarled. "Leave!"

Penelope and Kaya stared back defiantly.

"Okay, then." Massie flipped the power switch on the thin microphone clamped to the side of the altar. She leaned forward and pressed her glossed lips against it. "Kaya peed in her sleeping bag at my third-grade birthday party! And Penelope once sneezed during synchronized swim and—"

"Okay, fine!" Penelope took off faster than the cowardly lion in *The Wizard of Oz*. And Kaya was right behind her.

The girls exploded with laughter until Claire's cell rang.

"Is it Cam?" Massie wiped her tear-soaked cheeks.

"Yup," Claire said before checking the screen. Her tingling feet were never wrong. "Hullo?" She jumped off the stage.

"Hey." He sounded like he was jogging or pacing. "What's wrong? Did you make your decision? Are you moving?"

"What?" Claire's blond eyebrows practically smashed together. "No. Why?"

"You called like three times and I got worried."

"Oh." Claire felt an overwhelming need to touch his shoulder. "I just wanted to ask you something."

He sighed. She could hear his relief.

Massie gave Claire the hurry-up-and-get-on-with-it hand signal.

"Um." She walked up the steps to the stage. "I was thinking, uh, maybe we could come over tonight."

"We?"

Claire walked down the steps.

"Yeah." She looked at Massie, her wide blue eyes screaming for help. *"We."*

"Soccer lessons," Massie mouthed.

Kristen rolled her eyes.

"We want soccer lessons." She hated lying to him, and wondered if he sensed her blushing. "'Cause we're joining the OCD Sirens."

"Sure." He laughed. "But I can't tonight."

"Why?" Disappointment spread through Claire's body like a wave of prickly heat. And would rage through Massie's like a brush fire.

"I have a science test first period tomorrow and if I don't get a B-plus or higher, I'll—"

"We'll only be there for a few minutes," Claire heard herself whine.

Massie stomped her foot, obviously sensing the outcome. "Make him say yes."

"How about tomorrow?" Cam asked, sounding hopeful.

"Uhhhh, hold on, I'm losing my signal," Claire lied again. Once she was by the chapel doors, she said, "That's better," much louder than she needed to. Then she turned in toward her phone. "I can't tomorrow," she whispered. "I'll be in Manhattan, meeting with my agent. What about Thursday?"

"Soccer practice."

"Oh." Claire bit her thumbnail.

"How about Friday?" he offered.

"Are you sure you can't do tonight?"

"I wish I could, but—"

"That's okay, I understand." Claire didn't have to look up to know that the Pretty Committee was surrounding her. She could hear them whispering and shushing one another. "See you Friday."

"Bye."

Claire said goodbye in her head, but in reality she just hung up the phone.

"Friday?" Massie snapped. "That's the soonest we can get in there? What if someone else gets there first?" She gestured to the pews where Kaya and Penelope had been hiding.

"He has to study tonight." Claire's entire body felt heavy.

"What about tomorrow?"

"Uh, his uncle is visiting." She lied a third time. But she couldn't bear the thought of the girls at Cam's house without her. What if he realized that Massie was cooler than she was? Or that Alicia was prettier? Or that Dylan was funnier? Or that Kristen was a better athlete?

But then again, what if Massie knew that Claire's insecurities were keeping them from finding the key? Could anything be worse than that? There was no easy way out of this.

All Claire could do was lift her eyes toward the stained-glass dome above her head and pray for the best.

The morning sun reflected off the metal bleachers, creating random puddles of gold light where the Pretty Committee usually sat and flirted with the Briarwood soccer team. Sure, the soccer stadium looked nice enough at this hour, even inspiring, like those motivational sports posters in the guidance counselor's office about *achieving* success and not just dreaming about it.

But still, it was insanely early, and Massie couldn't help feeling disappointed with herself. Yes, she'd *promised* Principal Burns she'd join the OCD Sirens and learn to become a team player. It was either that or a lifetime of lunching with muffin-money-stealing juvies in public school. But it was only a *promise*, and Massie Block was a master at weaseling out of *those*. Yet here she was—chilly, groggy, and wearing cleats.

"Hey, you guys." Kimmy Rosen ran across the field toward the Pretty Committee. "Where did you get those uniforms?" She pushed her round Arthur the Aardvark glasses up the bridge of her narrow nose when she finally caught up. "I, like, completely want one for my birthday party next weekend."

Massie puffed out her chest and smiled. "Thanks, I designed them myself."

"They're couture." Alicia stroked her long dark ponytail extension.

"Socc-outure." Dylan giggled.

Kristen rolled her eyes.

"Can I order one?" Kimmy pulled up her regulation knee-high white socks. "I'm so sick of the whole navy-shorts-and-baggy-yellow-shirt thing."

"I *like* them." Kristen pulled her heel to her butt, stretching a hamstring. She looked to her teammates for support but got none. The gathering Sirens were forming an envy circle around Massie, Alicia, and Dylan to get a closer look at their creations. "Our uniforms are practical. Unlike *those*."

"These are more than practical. They're pract-*able*." Massie paused. "Practical and ah-dorable."

"Point."

It was one thing for Kristen not to wear one of Massie's special-edition uniforms, but it would be quite another for her to criticize them in public. Especially since Massie, Alicia, and Dylan were the only three girls on the field who actually looked female.

Their navy shorts had been ripped open by Massie's housekeeper, Inez, and sewn into A-line miniskirts. Cleavage-baring cuts transformed their boyish yellow tops into sexy V-necked tanks. And their boring white knee-highs had been cut into "sweat bangles" and moved to their wrists. Now the girls sported cute little tennis socks with fluffy lemon yellow pom-poms flopping around the heels of their cleats, introducing their harsh black sneakers to this spring's biggest "it" color. But the pièces de résistance were the numbers on their backs, which Inez had filled in with navy glitter. Massie put a hand on her waist—one foot out, and toes pointed—giving Kimmy and the other Sirens a moment to study the Pretty Committee's fabulousness. Alicia and Dylan did the same.

"Can I order one?" asked Marta Williams, who was known for wearing a white do-rag over her unruly brown curls.

"Me too," added Jessi Rowan before crouching to tighten her black laces.

"Everyone give Dylan your sizes and I'll see what I can do," Massie announced, with an I-told-you-so smirk aimed at Kristen.

"What happened to Siren pride?" Kristen asked her teammates as they formed a line in front of Dylan.

"What happened to *female* pride?" Massie answered for them. "The boys are practicing a few yards away." She pointed to the Briarwood Tomahawks, who were racing up and down the field, caught up in their morning drills. Uneasiness pinched her heart when she saw Derrington snaking around a row of orange pylons. Had he really lip-kissed Skye Hamilton? Quickly, Massie turned away, before full-blown sadness crept in and ruined her day.

Kristen opened her mouth to speak, but Coach Davis beat her to it.

"Line up," announced the petite blonde in an old 2003 black Juicy Couture sweat suit, white clouds of air puffing from her wide mouth.

Instead of moving, the girls stayed where they were and continued shouting their sizes at Dylan.

"Line!" Her perfectly even teeth practically morphed into fangs. "Now!"

The Sirens scurried into formation, a single row facing her. Massie edged out Kori Gedman, who was jockeying for a place beside Kristen, then grabbed Alicia and Dylan and pulled them beside her.

"How 'bout a strong Sirens welcome to Massie Block, Alicia Rivera, and Dylan Marvil?" The coach clapped her hands in a rhythmic staccato beat. Massie wondered if she had some sort of weird nerve disorder that prevented her from clapping like a normal, healthy person, until fifteen other girls joined in. Massie found their warm welcome more energizing than her morning Red Bull.

"Thank you," Massie mouthed.

She glanced over at the Tomahawks, hoping Derrington would notice the team applauding her. But he was busy inside the net, blocking the hailstorm of balls being kicked at his face.

Alicia nudged her "When should tell the coach I don't run?"

"I have a feeling she'll figure it out." Dylan fake-coughed while she opened a Ziploc baggie stuffed with bagel chips. Coughing again, she popped one in her mouth and held the bag out to her friends. "Carb-loading is the key to endurance."

"Shhhhh," Kristen hissed, never taking her eyes off the coach.

"We have high hopes for you girls," smiled the coach. Her wide green eyes glistened like sparkling sea glass against her bronzed skin. If she'd traded in her vintage sweat suit for a modern Azzedine Alaïa gown, she'd have looked like a red-carpet regular or an *E.T.* correspondent.

Assuming the adoration ran both ways, Massie imagined herself being crowned captain by the end of the week in a torchlight ceremony where they'd present her with a platinum soccer ball for her charm bracelet, or a tiny cleat. Something deep inside her shifted. Maybe she *could* learn to love a sport. All she'd have to do was score a few goals and then those silver seats would be filled with hundreds of people, shouting her name and cheering her on. And what wasn't to love about that?

"And I am doubly pleased to announce that our *star*, Kristen Gregory, is back at OCD after a devastating three-week expulsion. And that means we finally have a shot at the finals!"

The Sirens lifted Kristen into the air like she had already won the big game. Their cheers were *American Idol* loud. Much louder than they had been for Massie, Alicia, and Dylan. Of course, this time Derrington and the boys stopped practicing and looked.

Despite her frustration, Massie smiled and laughed so Derrington would think she preferred *not* to be the one getting carried around like royalty.

When the boys turned away, Massie smoothed out her

mini and whispered to Dylan, "Who knew Kristen was so 'in' with the SLBRs?"

"Soccer losers beyond repair?"

Massie nodded, unable to turn away from her Kristen-obsessed teammates.

Each time they lifted their "star," Massie felt more and more like a foreign-exchange student or a substitute teacher. Forget the platinum ball and the tiny cleat! Soccer, she suddenly decided, was for people who couldn't afford to shop.

Puuuuuuuuuur-uuurp!

Coach Davis's silver whistle put a much-needed end to the ah-nnoying fandemonium.

"Today we're going to practice dribbling and kicking." She paced the line, her eyes hardening with every step. "We're up against the Woodson Meerkats on Sunday. Beat them and we're off to the finals." She lifted her palm, blocking their cheers. "Their offense is strong. So this week we are going to focus on—"

Alicia raised her hand.

"Yes?"

"If I want to score a goal, where should I stand?"

Muffled giggles erupted.

The coach glared at Kristen, who had assured her the girls could hold their own on the field. "You're joking, right?"

Kristen pinched Alicia's elbow.

"Uh, yeah, totally."

Everyone laughed.

The coach shook her head, then continued. "I am going to use today's practice to evaluate our new players, which may mean different positions for some of you, depending on their strengths."

A few girls groaned.

Massie glanced at Alicia and Dylan, wondering if this whole thing felt like a dream to them too. They were both biting their nails. *Evaluate our new players? Different positions? Strengths?* Did Coach Davis not understand that the closest Massie had ever come to playing soccer was the time she'd kicked Livvy Collins's Hello Kitty pencil case into the male teachers' bathroom? If this *was* a dream, Massie prayed her clock radio would go off in the next five seconds and JoJo's new song would wake her before any embarrassing evaluating could begin.

Peeking to her right, Massie saw Cam sprinting, with five other guys. The sight of him made her instantly resent Claire. How hard could it have been to get invited to his house? What had made her settle on Friday, four whole days away? And why didn't Massie just call him herself?

"Um, I have a question." Dylan twirled a red ringlet around her finger. "How many calories are burned during a typical practice?" She crunched down on a bagel chip, emitting a cloud of garlic fumes.

Kristen tugged on her yellow Puma wristband.

"Good question, Miss Marvil," deadpanned the coach.

"Why don't you run across the field five times and we'll see if those shorts of yours don't get a little looser?"

"Actually, it's a skirt," Dylan offered.

"You don't say?" The coach's eyes softened. A now-why-didn't-you-tell-me-that-sooner look replaced her scowl. "Come forward and give us a look."

Dylan threw her hands above her head and twirled.

Kristen chewed the end of her side braid.

"Massie? Alicia?" The coach beckoned.

They stepped forward too.

The Sirens whooped and hollered with delight. Massie blew them kisses. It felt good to have them back.

"Forget about running across the field," said Coach Davis with a calming grin.

Dylan slapped her heart. "Thank you so mu—"

"See those towels over there by the bench?"

"Uh-oh," Kristen groaned.

"Take off those ridiculous party outfits, cover up in those towels, and then join our drill. Failure to do so in four minutes will result in this entire team sitting out Sunday's game."

Everyone gasped.

You're jealous of our creativity! You're a power-hungry failure! You're just upset you didn't think of glitter numbers first! Massie wanted to shout. But the coach beat her to it.

"Go!" She set the timer on her black Seiko stopwatch.

As long as all eyes were on her, Massie had to make whatever she was doing seem like the most fun ever, even if it involved public humiliation and a dew-covered soccer field.

So she giggle-jogged all the way to the bench. Thankfully, owing to a lifetime of slipping out of wet bathing suits at the beach, the girls were able to strip under their towels without incident.

"Woo-hooo," Massie yelped when her bare feet touched the cold grass. "Chilllllyyyyy," she shouted, just loud enough for Derrington to hear.

He stepped out of the net and shielded his eyes from the sun.

"Ew!" Alicia giggled. "What are *you* looking at?"

"A lot!" Derrington held out his hands like a zombie.

The boys high-fived him.

He wiggled his butt.

"Two minutes," the coach called.

"Ooops, my towel is slipping," Dylan joked.

The guys whistled.

"Claire is going to be so upset she missed this." Massie scraped some navy glitter off her #2 and sprinkled it over her bare collarbone.

"Fifty-three seconds," shouted the coach.

The boys whistled more.

"My dad is so suing for public humiliation." Alicia folded her arms across her chest.

"Why?" Dylan shimmied for the boys and got more whistles. "This is great!"

Massie considered racing over to Cam and asking if they could visit sooner, but Coach Davis shouted, "Twenty seconds!" before she had the chance.

"Hurry," their teammates urged.

"SLBRs," Massie muttered under her breath.

They scooped up their clothes and padded across the field like starlets at a day spa.

"Make us lose and you're dead," Kori hissed as she zipped past them kicking a ball.

"Impossible. You're already losers," Massie snapped.

The coach cupped her hands around her mouth and yelled, "Grab a ball and start dribbling!"

Dylan shoved one last bagel chip in her mouth, then dropped the crumb-filled bag on the field.

"Hey, Dylan, are you a cat?" asked Massie.

"No." She chewed.

"Then what's with the litter?"

Dylan was about to pick up the bag when Kori head-butted a ball toward her stomach. Along came another. Then another.

"Watch it!" Alicia squealed when one skimmed her cheek.

"Oops." Kori raced past them again, her posture so bad it looked like someone had kicked a ball into her stomach.

"Kori, look out!" Jessi shouted.

But it was too late.

The heel of her cleat came down on the Ziploc and she skidded across the field, landing smack on her kneecap.

"Owwwww!" She rocked back and forth cradling her leg.

"They should call those things Slip-locs." Massie giggled.

Dylan burst out laughing.

A crowd formed around Kori, and Massie knew it was now or never. "Cover me," she whisper-shouted.

"Where are you going?" Alicia whisper-shouted back.

"Cam!"

Massie gripped her towel and darted across the field.

It wasn't long before Kori's wailing faded and the sound of boys shouting, "Pass!" and "Quit hogging!" got louder. So what if she wasn't the MVP? Sprinting to the boys' side, half-nude during practice was sure to earn her a place in the soccer hall of fame.

"Toga party?" asked Cam. Luckily, he was sitting on the sidelines alone, tightening his laces.

"Long story." Massie blushed, suddenly feeling ten times more naked without her friends. "Listen, I just wanted to make sure Claire spoke to you about soccer lessons."

"Yeah, Friday night. Right?"

Two guys in matching burgundy shorts and green shirts whizzed past them.

"Right. But as you can see"—she clutched her towel—"we're not doing so well."

He snickered.

"So, can we come tonight? You know, after your uncle leaves?"

"My uncle?"

Puuuuuuuuuuur-uuurp! Puuuuuuuuuuur-uuurp!

Massie had no idea if that whistle was for her or Cam. And she didn't care. All that mattered right now was checking Harris's mattress as soon as possible.

"Fisher!" roared a stocky bald man in a silver-and-blue Nike track suit. "Let's go!"

Cam looked over his shoulder and locked eyes with his angry coach. "Uh-oh."

"What about Thursday?" Massie pleaded. "Can we come Thursday?"

"Why do so many girls want to come to my house lately?" Cam mussed his sweaty dark hair.

"What? What do you mean so many girls? Who?"

"Fish-er!" yelled the coach.

"I really gotta go." Cam jogged toward the coach. "See you Friday."

"Cam, wait! What girls? What did you tell them?"

But Cam was gone, leaving Massie wrapped in a nubby white towel in the middle of the soccer field, with nothing to kick but herself.

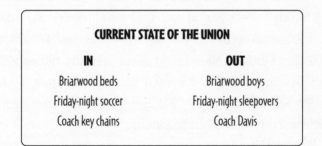

CURRENT STATE OF THE UNION

IN	OUT
Briarwood beds	Briarwood boys
Friday-night soccer	Friday-night sleepovers
Coach key chains	Coach Davis

Miles Baime's dark eyes followed a leggy brunette as she crossed the elegant champagne-colored dining room at the Four Seasons Hotel.

"I'm gonna get straight to the point," said Claire's boyishly handsome, dark-haired agent. "You have MSP!"

"She has *what*?" Judi Lyons whipped off her cherry-red bifocals.

"MSP." He leaned forward, clinking his gold knot cuff links against the marble tabletop, and folded his tanned hands. "Major. Star. Potential."

"Oh." Claire sighed, relieved. "It sounded like a disease."

"Hardly." Reaching across Claire's blueberry pancakes, he grabbed her wrist. "If you tap into it, the world is yours."

Claire blushed. Something about her too-cute-in-a-suit agent telling her how talented she was in front of her mother was embarrassing. Flattering and ego boosting and tingle worthy, but still embarrassing.

Finally, Miles let go.

Claire hid her hand on her lap and made a mental note to get her mom's permission to shave above the knee. She was wearing an American Eagle camouflage cargo minidress, and her pale exposed thighs felt like Astroturf.

"So you think my daughter has MSP?" Judi giggled at her use of such a hip Hollywood term. It was the first time she'd smiled all morning. Nervous that the film industry was out to exploit her only daughter, Judi had been skeptical but supportive about the move out west ever since Miles had suggested it three days earlier.

"Absolutely." He sank back into his wing chair. "In fact, Bernard Sinrod wants her for the lead in his new feature, *Princess Nobody*—"

Claire gasped. "No way! He's won, like, two Oscars."

"Four."

"And he wants *my* daughter?" Judi asked.

Claire sent a high-speed thanks-for-the-vote-of-confidence glare at her mother, who fired back with a can-you-blame-me shrug.

"He's seen an advance screening of *Dial L for Loser* and thinks your daughter would be perfect as the lead." Miles grinned. "It's about a scrappy NYC runaway who helps the prince of Bhutan after he's been mugged by street thugs. They fall in love and she ends up becoming a beautiful princess. And guess who's on board to play Prince Aroon?"

Claire's mind went blank. This was happening too fast. An A-list director wanted *her* to star in his next movie . . . as a princess! A beautiful one! She squeezed her cell phone under the table, wishing the Pretty Committee could listen in.

"Give up?" Miles flipped open his Razr and responded to a text message.

Claire nodded as fast as she could.

"Cole Sprouse," he announced. "You know, that mischievous blond twin from the Disney show *Suite Life of Zack and Cody*."

"Ehmagawd, I love him!" Claire beamed, imagining a cover photo on *US Weekly* of their blond heads pressed together in a friendly embrace.

"The money is decent and it shoots in Manhattan from June through August."

"Wonderful." Judi traced her mouth with Revlon's Rose Wine lipstick, then snapped the cap back on. "What a relief."

"So I can stay in New York for the summer?"

"Yup."

Claire poked her finger in the whipped cream swirl atop her short stack and popped it in her mouth. The sugar, mixed with the good news, gave her an instant rush. Excitedly, she kicked her mom under the table. It was going to be a perfect summer.

Every afternoon, Cam could visit her on the set. When she had a scene to shoot he could hang in her trailer and play video games. They'd become buddies with Cole, and the three of them could go to the Empire State Building and Coney Island and free concerts in Central Park. On the weekends she'd hang out with the Pretty Committee and swim in the Blocks' pool and ride her bike to Layne's and get ice cream and—

Miles knocked Claire's fattening whipped cream into a pool of maple syrup with a butter knife. "Runaways are thin."

Claire blushed again.

"Of course, the final act will be shot in Bhutan, so you will be spending most of the fall over there. But the people there are very kind." He signaled the waiter for the check. "Did you know their national sport is archery?"

Claire felt as if one of their national arrows had just embedded itself in her chest.

"*Most* of the fall?"

"Where is Bhutan?" asked Judi.

"Somewhere near India. Or is it Tibet?" He waved his Razr. "I'll have my assistant call you with an exact location. Don't worry; wherever it is, it'll be five-star all the way. "

Judi stabbed a grape from her fruit cup.

"Will I have to *live* there?"

"*If*"—Miles signed the check without looking at the total—"and only *if* you nail the audition."

Claire stiffened. She'd forgotten the part wasn't hers yet and hoped she hadn't come across as ungrateful. "What do I have to do?"

"Bernard is insisting you show up in character. That means you have to transform yourself into a scrappy, unkempt runaway. I'm talking choppy black hair, dirty fingernails, and eyebrow extensions."

"*Huh?*" Claire and Judi exclaimed together.

"Bernard is tired of the whole loser-takes-off-her-glasses-and-becomes-a-goddess cliché. He wants to give his audience something more extreme. And believe it or not, he found someone who can sew goat hair right into the eyebrows to make them coarse, bushy, and one. I'm telling you, the man's a genius. And he wants *you*."

Claire peeked at her reflection in the side of a silver teapot, trying to imagine herself a brunette with goat-hair-enhanced brows. And all she could picture was the Count from *Sesame Street*.

"Can't I wear a wig?"

"That's a great idea." Judi clapped. "And we can fill in your blond eyebrows with dark pencil. L'Oreal makes a great one called Prestige."

"Not happ-nin'." Miles wagged his finger. "Bernard wants to know that Claire is willing to commit to this role inside and out."

"What about school? Everyone will make fun of—"

"There are a million blondes in the greater Los Angeles area—not to mention Texas—willing to alter their appearance for the craft."

"Yeah, but—" Claire stabbed a dry, whipped-cream-free pancake.

"But nothing." Miles stuffed the yellow receipt in his breast pocket. "If you want to reach single-name status, you'll be back here, in the penthouse, Friday night at seven o'clock covered in more dark hair than the floor at Supercuts."

"*This* Friday?"

"Yup."

"Claire, you don't have to do this." Judi touched her daughter's icy hand. "There will be other opportunities. Other directors who will want you just the way you are."

"It's not *that*," Claire insisted, not bothering to explain that she was supposed to go to Cam's on Friday night to look for the key. And now, if she agreed to the audition, her friends would be there without her. Making memories, creating inside jokes, and smelling her boyfriend's Drakkar Noir–soaked neck.

"I'll be right back." Claire dropped her phone in her cargo pocket and pushed back from the table. It wasn't too late to call Cam from the bathroom and beg him to reschedule. "I just need a second to think about it."

"You have until I finish my coffee." Miles lifted the tiny espresso cup to his lips and then tilted his head back. He replaced the cup in the saucer with a dainty clink and let out a satisfied, "Ahhhh."

Then he looked directly into Claire's eyes and folded his arms across his chest.

"What's it gonna be?"

"Ah-nnoying!" Massie snapped her Motorola shut and knocked her head against the silver Range Rover's window. "Voice mail again!"

"Maybe she's on an airplane, flying to L.A.," Alicia offered as she picked a random piece of glitter off her lavender knit sweater. "Ugh! My soccer uniform leaked in my bag," she complained to no one in particular.

"I bet she's at the Keds factory with Mischa Barton designing a pair of signature geek-sneaks." Dylan plunked her legs down on Alicia's lap. "By the way, you never commented on my new black Paige jeans. Is it 'cause they make me look fat?"

"Get your meat sticks offa me!"

Kristen giggled.

"This is *serious*, you guys." Massie opened the window, hoping the cool breeze might calm her. But all it did was mess her hair. "Claire needs to tell Cam not to let any girls in his house." She repositioned her gray satin headband.

"Yul ee er ah ome." Dylan chewed a powdered Munchkin.

"Huh?"

She swallowed.

"I said, you'll see her at home." She reached into the

wax-lined Dunkin' Donuts bag and popped another round white-sugar-covered doughnut ball in her mouth. "Let's watch the news."

Isaac, Massie's driver, hit a button, and a flat-screen TV lowered from the ceiling.

Kristen's narrow aqua eyes widened. "Do you think something happened to her?"

"No." Dylan picked up the thin remote and flipped through the channels. "I saw a commercial last night about depression. It said one of the symptoms is loss of appetite. So maybe if I hear a sad story I'll stop eating these." She stuck a glazed doughnut ball in her mouth.

"Here's a sad story for you." Massie looked directly into Dylan's jade-colored cat eyes. "If I don't get in touch with Kuh-laire, I can't tell her to ask Cam which girls have been trying to get into his house. And if I don't know who they are, I can't stop them. If I can't stop them, they'll get the key first. And if they get the key first, we're done. And if we're *done,* eighth grade is going to feel like one long soccer practice."

Dylan bit into a chocolate Munchkin. "Not sad enough."

"It will be when Heather and her alt.com friends are the new alphas," Massie barked. "Better get used to cheap black sweaters and fake silver jewelry that'll turn your skin green."

She buried her face in her hands.

"Mass." Alicia's warm hand was on her back. "That key is so ours. Do you aw-nestly think Skye would let that room fall into LBR hands? Puh-lease! She's just testing us."

Massie lifted her head and gazed into Alicia's big brown eyes. They shimmered with quiet confidence.

"You think?"

"I know."

"Ah-greed." Dylan wiped her mouth on the sleeve of her L.A.M.B. bike-chain cardigan.

"I bet we're the only ones who got the CD-ROM," Alicia blurted.

"Then how do you explain Kaya and Penelope in the chapel?"

"Puh-lease." Alicia waved away her comment. "Those LBRs probably go there every day after school and pray for coolness."

"Ehmagawd, you're probably right." Massie swept the bangs away from her eyes. "I can't believe I fell for it."

"I can," Kristen blurted.

Her snippiness shocked Massie like a surprise hair tug. "Are you still mad we wore those soccer uniforms? Because that has *nothing* to do with—"

"No." Kristen rolled down her window. "You fell for it because it's true. Look."

The girls unclipped their seat belts and scrunched up beside her.

"Buckle up!" Isaac called from the front seat.

"Okay," Massie called sweetly, then turned back to the window.

Layne, Heather, and Meena were gathered outside Marc Cooper's modest brick house with fistfuls of silver helium balloons that said MARC IS #1 in blue bubble letters.

"Ehmagawd, they're wearing cheap black sweaters and faux silver." Alicia giggled.

"Stop the car!" Massie shouted.

Isaac screeched to a halt. "What is it?"

"Kristen, come with me." Massie grabbed her wrist and yanked her toward the open door.

"Where are we—?"

"Can I go too?" Alicia whined.

"No. I need someone who can run."

"Point." She closed the door.

Kristen, who was at least two paces ahead of Massie, led the charge as they bolted across the street to the Coopers' house. Under any other circumstances, Massie would have made her slow down and follow, but protocol be damned. This was an emergency.

"What are you guys doing here?" panted Massie when they reached the porch. "I didn't know you were friends with Marc."

"Oh, yeah." Heather slid a silver serpent charm back and forth across her tarnished chain necklace. "We're tight."

Layne pushed the doorbell again.

"Why are *you* here?" Meena twirled her one random chunk of dyed green hair.

Kristen glanced at their balloons. "To congratulate Marc."

"For what?" Layne tested.

"For being number one," Massie said with major amounts of "duh!" in her tone.

Finally, the door opened. The noxious smell of wet paint seeped out.

"Congratulations, Marc!" Shoving the balloons into his pale, smooth hand, Heather forced herself inside. She charged up the stairs without another word.

Massie shoved Kristen into the house, knowing the infamous soccer star had a decent shot at overtaking her. "Hurry!"

"Where are you going?" Marc whimpered, twisting the bottom of his spaghetti-sauce-stained gray tee around his finger.

Massie took off behind Kristen, successfully outrunning Layne and Meena.

Along the way, she passed dozens of framed photos. Various unflattering shots of the Afro twins—Marc and his sister, Karla—posed year after year on the same tree stump wearing matching mustard-yellow turtlenecks, in their woodsy backyard.

"Ehmagawd!" Kristen's voice echoed from one of the bedrooms.

The paint smell got stronger as Massie neared the top, but poisonous fumes couldn't keep her from the key. She hurried into the room.

Stained white drop cloths below freshly painted brown walls were the only things she found.

Meena and Layne burst through the door.

"Where's your bed?" Massie called to Marc, who ran into the room right after her.

"Hey, aren't you the girl from *The Daily Grind*?" he asked.

Massie smiled and nodded.

Kristen rolled her eyes.

"So?" Heather asked. "*Where* is it? Where's your bed and stuff?"

"In storage until the paint dries." Marc chewed his lower lip. "I've been crashing downstairs on the couch. It's cool, though, 'cause I can watch ESPN as late as I want."

Minutes later, Massie and Kristen were back in the Range Rover.

"I knew Marc didn't have the key," Alicia insisted. "That's why he's not on my list."

"How do you *know*?" Massie smacked the camel-colored leather seat.

"Skye never kissed him."

"How do you *know*?"

"I told you, I can't reveal my sources," Alicia insisted.

Massie rolled her eyes, "You could have told me that before I ran into his poisonous house."

"If I'd been with you, I would have."

"Ehmagawd, look!" Dylan stuffed another Munchkin in her mouth. "Olivia is on the back of Kemp Hurley's bike."

"They're pulling into his driveway!" Kristen announced.

With extreme urgency, Massie rolled down her window. "Hey, Olivia!"

The beautiful blonde turned and waved, flashing her perfect, never-needed-braces smile. "Hey!"

"How's the rash?" Massie called. "Did you get the ointment or are you still super itchy?"

Kemp stopped his bike.

"Massie!" Isaac sped up, obviously trying to avoid a run-in with the neighbors.

The girls erupted in hysterics as Olivia tore off down the pine-studded street.

After a sharp turn onto Candlenut Road, Kristen shouted, "Ehmagawd! There's Kori. She's on crutches."

Chris Plovert hopped beside her, using Strawberry's ample shoulder for support. His leg cast was wrapped in plastic because the dark clouds were threatening rain.

"There's no way the Slip-loc put her on crutches." Dylan's expression hung somewhere between surprise and laugher.

"It didn't," Massie insisted. "She's faking so she can go to Plovert's house. Don't you see? It's madness out there! Everyone's in the game but us." She stuck her head out the window. "Hey, Plovert, Alicia thinks you're hot!"

Alicia smacked Massie's thigh. "What are you doing?"

"Trust me."

Kristen cackled. Dylan laughed.

"Really?" Plovert called back.

"Swear. But she's really jealous."

Before they knew it, Plovert had reclaimed his crutches and was waving goodbye to Kori.

The girls held out their palms, ready to give Massie a much-deserving high five. But she denied them. This was far from over.

"Isaac, we need to stop at the corner of Maple and Birch."

He pulled into a wide circular driveway, turning the Range Rover around.

"You are nawt!" Dylan covered her mouth in shock.

"Am!" Massie unzipped her navy Prada makeup case, opened her Chanel No. 5, and dabbed a little behind her ears.

"It's against the rules," Kristen reminded her.

"Puh-lease, I doubt the rules apply to *us*." Massie swiped some glitter-infused Caramel Cream Glossip Girl on her lips and blotted on the inside cover of her science textbook. "Skye probably made up the whole don't-talk-to-me thing to keep the LBRs away. Any good alpha would have done the same."

"Point."

They turned onto Birch, parking across from a quaint A-frame colonial. The winding street was packed with average-size homes complete with two-car garages and enough front lawn for a game of five-person tag. Nothing more.

Massie grinned.

Her neighborhood was better than Skye's.

"Ehmagawd, there she is." Alicia sounded awestruck. "Wearing a ballet tutu over gray stovepipe jeans. I *heart* that."

"I like her beat-up jean jacket," Kristen noted. "There's a great juxtaposition thing going on there. The whole tough-meets-feminine thing."

"Whatevs." Dylan shoved yet another sprinkle-covered Munchkin in her mouth. "Our soccer uniforms were just as creative."

They watched in silence as Skye stepped off Liam Barrett's black Vespa. She unclipped her silver helmet, then finger-fluffed her just-got-back-from-the-beach sand-colored ringlets.

Massie kicked open the door. "I'm going in."

Alicia grabbed her wrist. "What are you going to say?"

"I'm gonna reason with her, alpha to alpha." Massie slipped off her gray Vince shrug so that her ah-dorable red Diane von Furstenberg wrap dress wouldn't go unnoticed.

Kristen crossed her fingers. "Good luck."

"Wait!" Dylan grabbed the sleeve of Massie's dress. "Take these." She tossed her the wax-coated bag of Munchkins. "Skye likes mini things, remember?"

Massie caught the bag, saluted her girls, and then headed out.

WESTCHESTER, NY
THE HAMILTON HOME
Tuesday, April 6th
4:36 P.M.

The clouds darkened to an eerie greenish gray as Massie marched across the street, moving through varying pockets of humid and cold air. Wind rustled the leaves on nearby trees, which at first sounded like someone whispering, "Shhhh." Was nature urging her to keep her mouth closed? She stopped walking and listened again. This time it sounded like applause, an obvious message to forge ahead.

The Hamilton home had a cheery vibe. The porch was surrounded by charmingly rusted wagons filled with wildflowers and smooth round rocks. Smoke puffed from the chimney, filling the neighborhood with the spicy warm smell of firewood. It reminded Massie of the ah-dorable Shire scene in *Lord of the Rings* (the only decent part of the whole snoozer of a movie). But truth be told, the whole thing was no bigger than her guesthouse—something Massie hoped Skye had noticed when she and her mysteriously hot, yellow-Porsche-driving friend were at the Block estate two days earlier.

At the top of the driveway, Skye and Liam were beside the Vespa, touching palms to see whose was bigger. Feeling like an LBR stalker, Massie reminded herself that the only *real* difference between her and Skye was age. If they were in the same grade, they would be BFFs. So why let some-thing as silly as a birthday intimidate her? After all, Skye would probably be psyched she'd stopped by.

"Hey, Skye." Massie charged up the driveway.

"Hey!" Skye removed her hand from Liam's and waved. Her crackly voice gave Massie the sudden urge for Rice Krispy Treats.

"I need to talk to you for a second." She paused. "In pri-vate."

Liam shrugged, then flicked a silver Hershey's Kiss wrapper onto the driveway. His wide hazel eyes were droopy with what Massie assumed was exhaustion.

"Let's go round back." Skye held up a finger, letting Liam know she'd only be a minute.

He adjusted his tan knit cap and shrugged again.

Massie beamed, thrilled with herself for trusting her instincts.

Skye, who walked with her feet out in first position, led the way in metallic green ballet flats that matched the storm clouds overhead. Massie tried to imitate her but instantly felt like a duck.

"So, what's up?" Skye touched the ivy-covered stone on the side of her house. Her left arm glided gracefully across her torso, skimming the neighbor's hedges, then drifted over her head like an arched feather. She pliéd twice, then rested in third position.

"Doughnut?" Massie held out Dylan's bag. "They're mini."

"Yummers!" Skye dug in and pulled out a sugarcoated ball. "I love mini things."

"Same!" Massie forced herself to bite into a Munchkin. The sugar rush made her jaw tighten.

After Skye swallowed, her smile faded. Her Tiffany-box-colored eyes darkened as she glared at Massie, like she had on the CD-ROM. "Why. Are. You. Here?"

A gust of cool wind blew through the shrubs like a 3,000-watt hair dryer over a Mohawk.

"Um, I, uh . . ." Massie's palms itched. The hedges felt like they were closing in on her.

"Well?"

"It's an alpha thing," Massie tried.

Skye reached into pocket of her jean jacket and pulled out a tiny heart-shaped mirror. Holding it up to her face, she said, "I only see one alpha." Then she held it up to Massie. "And one cheater. And you know what that means."

A clap of thunder interrupted her, and then the rain began to fall. First one drop, then another, and within seconds it sounded like hundreds of acrylic nail tips tapping nervously on a desk.

"Actually," Massie shouted above the rain, "I'm, uh, here to find out what you want for graduation."

"Really?" Skye tilted her head and folded her arms across her chest.

"Really," she stalled, desperate for a lightbulb moment.

"And why do *you* want to get me a graduation present?"

And then it hit her.

"Who said it was from me?"

Skye furrowed her blond brows.

"Can I trust you?"

The doubtful expression behind Skye's eyes softened. "Course."

Massie signaled her to come closer.

Clearly not into taking orders from a seventh grader, Skye angled her head, giving Massie an ear instead.

"Okay." Massie looked right. Then left. "But you can't say a word to anyone."

Skye crossed her heart, oblivious to the soaking rain.

Cupping her mouth, Massie leaned in toward Skye's ear. "The gift," she whispered, "is from an ah-dorable boy who sent me to find out what you want. That's why I'm here."

"Seriously?" Skye chirped. "Who is it? Who sent you?"

"Guess."

Massie's heart thumped in anticipation.

"Ehmagawd, is it—?" She quickly cut herself off.

"*Who?* Who were you going to say?" Massie pleaded, feeling certain the answer would lead her straight to the mystery mattress.

Skye's eyes hardened.

"No one."

As if noticing the rain for the first time, Skye shimmied out of her jean jacket and held it above her already drenched head, leaving Massie exposed. Something in her had shifted.

"A pony."

"Huh?" Massie dried her cheeks with the back of her hand.

"Tell *him* I want a pony for graduation. And if I don't get one, certain *other* people won't ever, ever, ever get what they want." She glared deep into Massie's eyes. "Know what I mean?"

For a split second Massie considered playing dumb. But Skye was obviously onto her, and it would have been *legitimately* dumb to anger her more.

A dizzying, falling sensation overcame Massie. It felt worse than an eyebrow wax. The pain lingered in ways that associated with ripping hair out of her face didn't.

"Don't worry, I'll tell him about the pony." Massie showed Skye her phone to prove it. "I'll call him as soon as I dry off."

"While you're at it, tell *him* to stop sending LISPs to do his dirty work." She put her hands on her hips. "That is, if *he* even exists."

Massie's ears buzzed. No one had ever called her a Little Insignificant Seventh-grade Pee-on before. No one had ever dared! Standing there, trapped under the hateful gaze of OCD's eighth-grade alpha, Massie didn't know whether to defend her honor or run.

If only she could highlight the last ten minutes and delete them. She'd drive straight past Skye's *Lord of the Rings* house and spend every waking moment trying to find subtle yet effective ways to show Skye that she was the opposite of a LISP. And prove that she was a rich, beautiful, clever, stylish comeback queen. But that opportunity was long gone.

"Why are you still here, LISP?"

Fat drops of rain beat down on her like angry punches. "I'm nawt." Lifting her gray Rafe bag above her head, Massie dashed down the driveway, unable to stop herself from running like an LBR. She kicked Liam's silver foil across the soaked driveway, then whipped the soggy Dunkin' Donuts bag into the trash bin by the curb. She'd failed in her mission, a mistake so grave it could cost the Pretty Committee the key.

"Tell us everything, and don't leave one thing out," Alicia squealed when Massie dove into the backseat. "Did she tell you our dance instructor gave me a star for my pas de bourrée last week?"

"She wants us to win, right?" Kristen asked.

"Where's the key?" Dylan burped.

Everyone laughed, except Massie, whose mood was further agitated by the sting of the air-conditioning on her wet skin.

"Dylan, is my name Dorothy?"

"Uh, no."

"Then why did you think Munchkins could help me?"

They cracked up again while Massie stared out the window at the long wet road ahead, wondering how she was going to buy a pony without her parents finding out.

CURRENT STATE OF THE UNION

IN	OUT
Big mistakes	Little doughnuts
Graduation pony	Graduation party
Stormy Skyes	Sunny skies

Claire closed the door of the bronze Ford Taurus as quietly as she could. Judi did the same. They tiptoed across the gravel driveway toward the stone walkway that sliced through the Blocks' lawn and led to the guesthouse.

"Let's go." Judi held her black Talbots tote bag above her head. "It's dark and raining and—"

"Shhhh," Claire hissed. "Run ahead if you want, just don't make any noise."

"Claire, you're being ridiculous."

"Shhhhh." Claire ducked down.

"Suit yourself!" Judi scurried toward home, leaving her daughter behind in the rain.

Just as Claire had feared, the lights were on in the horse-shed-turned-spa.

They were in there.

If she could only sneak past the windows undetected. From there it would be a quick sprint and just two flights of stairs to the safety of her bedroom.

An urgent text message vibrated on Claire's cell phone. **911 meeting in GLU headquarters**, it said. Which really meant Girls Like Us headquarters, which really really meant the spa.

Pushing her black oversize wannabe-Dior sunglasses up her nose and securing her Faux-ch (fake Coach) plaid bucket hat (thank heavens for Times Square vendors and their cheap designer knockoffs), Claire assumed the crouch'n'dash position. She was about to make a run for it when someone shouted, "Hey, Nicole, I loved you on *The Simple Life 4*!"

She froze.

"Looks like you're really embracing the whole Hollywood thing." Dylan snickered. She was wearing a Burberry trench coat and carrying a six-pack of Diet Dr Pepper and a black bag of Smartfood, obviously taken from the pantry in the main house. "Come on." She tilted her head toward the spa. "Massie's been texting you like crazy. Let's go."

Wiping her palms on the sides of her wet cargo minidress, Claire followed.

"After you," Dylan conceded when they reached the rustic barn door.

"Great," Claire murmured, sliding it open like the door of a minivan.

Inside, dozens of vanilla-scented candles cast a warm orange glow across the leather furniture and created long treadmill shadows against the rustic wood walls. The waterfall in the Zen rock garden trickled while the burning wood in the fireplace popped and crackled. Ceramic pots of bubbling chocolate fondue—surrounded by skewers of strawberries, bananas, and sponge cake—filled the room with a rich, sugary smell that made Claire's mouth water.

It felt more like one of Kendra Block's après-ski parties than a Pretty Committee meeting, until she saw the glass coffee table piled high with empty, gloss-stained Starbucks cups.

Without lifting her head, Massie handed Claire a stack of stapled papers. "Nice of you to show."

"What's going on?" Claire sat on the ottoman beside Massie's bare, French-pedicured feet. Obviously, no one cared enough to ask how her meeting with Miles had gone.

"Read."

Claire looked down, wishing she had been bombarded with what-are-you-wearing jokes. Something! But the girls were silent, making the document in her hands the only place Claire could turn.

She scanned the first page. It was a copy of the poem Skye had read on the CD-ROM. The rest was a grid that listed the boys she had kissed and the reasons they might have the key.

FOR PRETTY COMMITTEE EYES ONLY

The boy who sleeps atop the key
Is into the exact same things as me.
He loves all creatures, big and small,
So his age doesn't matter, not at all.
I try not to think about his "Glamour-don't" style
By focusing on his kick-butt smile.
Note to self: I've kissed this guy,
But I've kissed them all. How bad am I?

We already rode off into the sunset together,
But the next time we do, it will be forever.
Holla!

NAME/GRADE	WHY HIM?	OPERATIVE	TACTIC
Todd Lyons/5th	1. Skye kissed him. 2. "Age doesn't matter."	Claire	Home advantage. Go in whenever you can. Right, Kuh-laire????
Tiny Nathan/5th	1. Skye kissed him. 2. "Age doesn't matter." 3. "All creatures, big and *small*"—we don't call him Tiny for nuthin'.	Claire	You want to see his SpongeBob sheets because Todd loves them and you want to get him some for his birthday.
Derrington/7th	1. Skye kissed him (but he didn't kiss her back). 2. "'*Glamour*-don't' style"—shorts in winter.	Massie	I want to make sure his mattress tag is on because the tag actually says it's illegal to cut it off and I don't want him to get into trouble.
Chris Plovert/ 7th	Kori & Strawberry checked.	N/A	N/A
Kemp Hurley/7th	Duh-livia checked.	N/A	N/A
Doug Landsman/ 7th	Layne, Meena, and Heather checked.	N/A	N/A
Jake Shapiro/ 7th	1. Skye kissed him. 2. "Kick-butt smile"— dad owns Brite Smile franchise.	Dylan	Your teeth have been yellowing. Want to talk to his dad. Then go to the "bathroom" and check under his mattress.
Josh Hotz/7th	1. Skye kissed him (but he didn't kiss her back). 2. "'Glamour-don't' style"—100% Polo.	Alicia	Went to an RL sample sale and got him something. You want to display it and need a few minutes in his room alone to set up the surprise.

NAME/GRADE	WHY HIM?	OPERATIVE	TACTIC
Grier Biggs/8th	1. Skye kissed him. 2. "Loves all creatures, big and small"—his last name is Biggs.	Alicia	You heard his room was voted coolest boy's room by some of the 8th-grade girls and you want to see its winning qualities.
Lowell Katz/8th	1. Skye kissed him. 2. "All creatures, big and small"—had head lice and saved them in a jar.	Alicia	You want to see his lice. It's research for your science-fair project on bad-hair days.
Andy Walden/8th	1. Skye kissed him. 2. "Rode off into the sunset together"—gave Skye a ride on his BMX bike before last year's Valentine's Day dance.	Alicia	You heard he had cool bike posters in his bedroom and are seriously into BMX-ing ever since you saw that episode of *Made* on MTV where Warwick taught that blond actress girl how to ride a BMX bike.
Ezra Rosenberg/8th	1. Skye kissed him 2. "Into the same things as me"—loves mini golf. Had a mini-golf birthday party.	Kristen	You want help practicing on your golf swing because all athletes take up golf at some point in their lives.
Oliver Smalls/8th	1. Skye kissed him. 2. "Loves all creatures, big and small"—his last name is Smalls.	Alicia	Someone saw him stealing your cell phone. He will ahb-viously deny this, but tell him you don't believe him and you want to check his room.
Cody Hill/8th	1. Skye kissed him. (Ew! Not sure why. Maybe she lost a bet.) 2. That's all. Other than that he's a total LBR.	Dylan	Say anything. He is such an LBR he will be happy you want to hang out with him.
Geoff Michaels/8th	1. Skye kissed him. 2. "All creatures, big and small" and "into the same things as me"—gets rides to school in a Mini Cooper.	Kristen	You want to see his regional spelling bee award. You think spelling is hawt.

NAME/GRADE	WHY HIM?	OPERATIVE	TACTIC
Luis Ruiz/8th	1. Skye kissed him. 2. "Age doesn't matter"—he's really 11 but skipped two grades.	Dylan	You want to see where he does his homework.
P.J. Jeffries/8th	1. Skye kissed him. 2. "Rode off into the sunset together"—their parents are BFFs and took them on the Circle Line cruise around NYC during sunset last spring.	Kristen	You want to interview him for a paper you are writing about people who are named after girls' pajamas. (You are also interviewing Teddy Stark and Cami Logan.)
Billy Williams/ 8th	1. Skye kissed him. 2. Another LBR. Not sure why she kissed him. Possibly a game of spin-the-bottle.	Dylan	You like his red hair and think you may be related. Must discuss in private. (Wear gloves when touching his mattress. He smells like calamine lotion, which may indicate a rash.)
Lee Chan/8th	1. Skye kissed him. 2. "Loves all creatures, big and small"—has a massive Shrek doll in his bedroom. His father worked on the movie.	Kristen	You want to get your picture taken with Shrek.
Harris Fisher/ H.S.	1. Skye kissed him. 2. "Next time it will be forever." She is in love with Harris, according to Claire.	Massie, Claire, Dylan, and Alicia.	Claire, Dylan, and Alicia get soccer tips from Cam while Massie searches Harris's room.
Liam Barrett/ H.S.	1. Skye kissed him. 2. "We rode off into the sunset together"—he drives Skye home on his Vespa.	Alicia	You want a ride on his Vespa but first you have to change into your Vespa outfit (in his bedroom, of course).
Yuri Butterman (aka Yuri Butt-Man)/H.S.	1. Skye kissed him. 2. "Into the same things as me"—majorly into dancing (ballroom).	Alicia	You need to practice with a tall male partner.

"Why am I the operative on so many?" Alicia whined.

"Look down," Massie insisted.

Alicia lowered her head, practically resting her chin on her ample cleavage.

"Oh."

"If our tactics don't get your into their bedrooms, those will."

Alicia folded her arms across her chest while Dylan and Kristen cracked up.

Bzzzzzzz.

Massie, Alicia, Dylan, Kristen, and Claire checked their phones.

"It's me." Claire jiggled her cell. "It's a text message from my agent," she announced, hoping one of them would ask her how her meeting had gone. Instead, they all returned to their documents. She scrolled down to Miles's message, which said:

Remember, runaways don't eat.

It was the fifth one she'd gotten from him in the last three hours.

After another moment of fake reading, Claire worked up the nerve to suggest the unsuggestable. "So, um, here's an idea." Adjusting her black oversize sunglasses, she gazed into the distance as if considering this for the very first time. "Maybe we should bump the Harris Fisher visit to next week."

"Why would we make Harris *later*?" Massie countered. "If anything, we'd want to go there sooner."

"Uh, you know, so we can check out some of these other guys first." She shook the list for effect.

Everyone giggled.

"Kuh-laire, you *must* be poor."

"Why?"

"Cuz you're not making *any* cents."

Dylan spit out a mouthful of Diet Dr Pepper.

Kristen cackled. "I love that one!"

"Me too." Alicia smacked the gray-and-aubergine Indian wool blanket around her legs. Surrounded by the Blocks' rustic-chic leather furniture and lit by the orange glow of the fire, all she needed was a huge turquoise necklace to look like an exotic model in a Ralph Lauren catalogue.

Claire clenched her fists, resisting the urge to beat herself senseless. She had rehearsed her argument a million times on the car ride back from Manhattan. Why did she have to say the one thing that defied all logic?

"Kuh-laire, what's this *really* about?" Massie finally looked at her. "Is something bothering you?" She sounded like a concerned friend. And Claire couldn't help wondering if this was Massie's way of apologizing for not asking about her meeting with Miles. Maybe she had heard the pain in Claire's voice and opted to put their friendship before this stupid key contest. And if that was the case, the least Claire could do was return the gesture with a little honesty.

"I have an audition Friday night."

"For what?" Dylan stuffed a handful of Smartfood in her mouth. "Nicole Richie's understudy?"

"Yeah, what's with that getup?" Alicia giggled.

"Wait." Massie held up her palm, obviously ordering them to let Claire finish. "Go awn."

"Bernard Sinrod wants me to star in his new movie, *Princess Nobody,* with guess who?"

No one said a word.

"Give up?" Claire tried.

Still they were silent.

"Cole Sprouse!"

She waited for their screams.

"Whatevs. Dylan's cuter," said Dylan.

"They're identical twins," Kristen insisted.

"Well, his *name* is cuter."

What is wrong with you guys? I'm up for a major movie and all you care about is which Sprouse is cuter? Claire wanted to shout. Instead, she fell back on the couch and lowered the brim of her plaid hat.

"So you're saying you want us to change *our* plans with Cam, the ones *you* set up, so you can go to your movie audition?" Massie bobbed her bare feet in anger.

"Yeah," Claire tried.

"Puh-lease! When are you going to realize this has *nothing* to do with you and Cam and *everything* to do with our eighth-grade alphaness?"

Nervously, Claire folded the hem of her camo skirt. "I—"

"It's chaos out there, Kul-laire. Kay-aw-ssss!" Massie

pointed to the floor-to-ceiling windows. "While you were lunching with Planet Hollywood, every girl in our grade has been trying to score an invite to Cam's."

"Who?" Claire shot forward. "Why didn't anyone tell me?"

"Check your cell." Massie waved her Motorola. "I've been leaving you messages all day and you've been sending me straight to VM like I was some kind of LBR stalker."

Claire opened her mouth but nothing came out.

"I can explain," she finally managed.

"Don't bother." Massie rolled her eyes.

"Maybe she's too famous to answer her phone," Alicia suggested.

"Or maybe she can't hear it under that hat," Dylan said.

"Or see it from behind those glasses," Kristen added.

Claire stood and faced everyone. "Wanna know why I'm wearing this?"

They glared at her.

She tore off her disguise, revealing a head of goth-black hair that looked like it had been cut by the teeth of a wild dog and a dark, bristly five-inch eyebrow.

"That's why."

No one laughed. No one even smiled. All they did was stare.

Swallowing hard, Claire met their eyes and began: "The director wants me to wear this to the audition Friday to show how dedicated I am to the role."

They said nothing. No jokes, no giggles, no screams. Just silence.

"Ehmagawd. Kuh-laire, is that *you*?" Massie asked as if, after years, the two had just bumped into each other at Sephora.

"Who did you think it was?"

"*Hairy* Potter." Massie burst out laughing.

The Pretty Committee took cover behind a row of shrubs across the street from Briarwood Academy. Squatting, they scoped their marks.

"I have eyes on Josh." Massie racked focus on her ah-dorable palm-size camouflage binoculars, shading her lenses from the late-afternoon sun. "He's tying one of his silver Nikes by the army-guy statue. Go! Go! Go!"

Alicia sprang to her feet. After smoothing her wide-legged Ralph Lauren pants, she tucked her cleavage inside the ever expanding borders of her crisp white V-neck.

"Remember, five p.m. at Wrap Star to debrief. First one there gets the booth."

"Given." Alicia saluted. "GL."

"Good luck," they whispered back.

"Gawdspeed," Massie muttered as Alicia crossed Brook Street and raced toward her crush.

The thought of losing this contest made her legs weak. She needed to sit but wouldn't have dreamed of putting her gold silk Chanel shorts in contact with the moist grass. A single green skid mark or mud stain and all confidence would be lost. Instead, Massie shifted her weight from one bare knee to the other and prayed this would all be over soon.

"I can't see *anything*." Dylan smacked the manicured cube of leaves in front of them. "These stupid bushes are in the way."

"Kuh-laire, scoot back—your eyebrows are blocking our view."

Everyone burst out laughing.

"Very funny." Claire adjusted the stylish black Stella McCartney sunglasses and matching wide-brimmed chocolate-brown suede hat Massie had forced upon her.

"There's Ezra Rosenberg." Kristen lowered her yellow Radio Shack binoculars. "Time to work on my golf swing."

"You may want to get that letter out of your mailbox first." Dylan snickered.

"Oops." Kristen cackled as she pulled the olive-colored James Perse tube dress she wore from between her butt cheeks.

"There's Jake!" Massie shoved Dylan, knocking her onto the damp grass.

"Watch it." Dylan stood. "This is organza." She inspected her turquoise tunic for water damage.

"This is about your yellow teeth, not your outfit, remember?" Massie huffed. "You're there to talk to his dad about whitening treatments."

"Yup." She licked a lemon gumball and scraped it across her teeth. "Got it. See ya at five."

"Wait up!" Claire hurried to catch up with Dylan and Kristen. "I see Tiny Nathan."

Massie lifted her binoculars and scanned the crowded

campus, hoping Derrington would emerge soon. Getting caught alone in the bushes with a pair of binoculars could seriously damage a girl's reputation.

It wasn't long before she spotted the shaggy-haired blond wiggling his butt for a group of amused seventh-grade boys. They high-fived before parting ways on their bikes, them in various shades of tan khakis and him in blue plaid AE shorts.

The traffic light at the top of Brook Street must have turned green, because a row of cars zipped past, blocking Massie's view. By the time it cleared, Derrington was gone.

Immediately, she speed-dialed.

He answered after one ring.

"Block?"

"Hey." Massie glossed up with Glossip Girl Strawberry Milkshake. "Where are you?"

"Riding down Grove Street."

"Oh." Massie tried to sound disappointed.

"Why?"

"I'm across from the army guy. I was hoping you could double me." She shoved the tops of her argyle socks into her riding boots, buttoned her shrunken black blazer, and tugged her mocha Vince tank so that it kissed the white Hermès scarf she'd threaded through her belt loops. Standing, she flipped her hair and tapped her chilly thigh, congratulating herself on an outfit well put together.

"Where's Isaac?" Derrington asked, his voice strangely louder than it had been a second ago.

"Um, we're trying to conserve gas," Massie tried. "Not because we're poor, though. It's a green thing."

"Conservation is coooool," someone whispered, right in her ear.

"Ahhhh!" Massie whipped her head around to find Derrington bouncing on his silver BMX bike, laughing.

"Puh-lease, I knew you were there." She rolled her eyes, trying to conceal the Pop Rocks–style explosions she felt in her stomach every time she saw him.

Derrington smiled. "Jump on." He smacked the black seat.

In an effort to avoid lifting her leg like a dog (so gauche!), Massie straddled the back tire, then shuffled toward the seat like she had a pair of lacy Cosabellas around her ankles.

Derrington pushed off the curb. "Hold tight."

Massie gripped the cold metal bar, feeling like Skye on the back of Liam's Vespa.

Derrington quickly turned his head. "No, hold on to *me*."

"Oh." She pinched the back of his gray Briarwood blazer.

"Whoa!" Derrington spun to the left, then the right, then the left again.

"What are you *doing*?"

"You better hold on!"

"You're not scaring me!" she shouted, grateful that he couldn't see the terror in her eyes.

"I'm gonna keep doing this until you hold on!" He made another sharp left.

"Heeeelp!" she squeaked.

A sudden loss of balance—caused by the shifting makeup

and books in Massie's white Marc Jacobs calfskin tote—made her tip. Prickly, stinging sweat flooded her armpits.

"E-nufff!"

Derrington dragged his black Vans along the street and stopped.

"You okay?"

Hanging off the side, Massie dug her fresh manicure into the seat and pulled herself up.

"Uh-huh," she managed, despite how close she'd come to having her face exfoliated by Maple Boulevard.

"You gonna hold on this time or what?"

Massie took a deep breath and on the silent count of three wrapped her arms around Derrington's fat-free waist like someone who wasn't the least bit nervous to touch a boy.

"Better." He began pedaling.

They turned onto Oak Lane and Massie dropped her shoulders. The lush neighborhood reminded her of Galwaugh Farms with its serene, winding horse trails.

"Hang on!" Derrington tugged on the handlebars and jumped the bike onto the curb.

Massie tightened her grip—not because she was scared, but because she wasn't.

By the time they hit Cedar Walk they were practically slow dancing. Massie had to remind herself that she was on a mission.

"You live around here, don't you?"

"No," he shouted into the balmy breeze.

"Oh. I can't believe I don't know where you live."

"Yes, you do, you came over two years ago on Halloween, remember? Dylan slipped on a smashed pumpkin and spilled her candy?"

"I don't think I was there," Massie lied, remembering dozens of kids descending on the candy while Dylan fought them off with white pebbles from Derrington's garden. "And I hate that I can't picture where you sleep."

Derrington stopped pedaling. "Wanna come over?"

"Sure." Massie smiled behind his back.

"'Kay." He turned the bike around.

"So, um, what do you think of Skye Hamilton?" Massie asked once they picked up speed.

"She's okay, I guess. Why?"

"I heard a rumor." She held her breath, fearing his response.

"Oh yeah?" he perked up. "What?"

"Just that you lip-kissed her." Massie tried to sound casual and unjealous.

"How'd you hear that?"

"So it's true!"

"Are you jealous?"

"Are you admitting it?"

"Jealous?"

"Admitting?"

Massie flicked an imaginary piece of hair off her sleeve, hoping to hide her disappointment.

"So what *happened*?"

Derrington faced her. He looked like an ah-dorable dopey golden Lab.

"This."

He leaned in, accidentally pressing his cold lips against her left nostril.

Massie raised her head, letting him know it was okay to try again.

This time he got her freshly glossed lips.

Massie lifted her arm and rested it lightly on his shoulder. The wool from his blazer was rough, but the rest of Derrington was surprisingly tender. Cars whooshed past, their engines sounding muted and distant, like Massie was wearing headphones or a fluffy winter hat. She felt light and warm and tingly, suspended in a place where it didn't matter what the drivers might be thinking of her outfit or her hair or her kissing technique or her boyfriend.

And for the next forty-one seconds, those feelings stayed with her.

Once the GG Strawberry Milkshake gloss had worn off, Massie knew it was time to pull back. Dry kissing was like eating a veggie burger with no condiments. It lacked flavor.

"So you kissed Skye like *that*?" She hid behind a wall of long, razored bangs.

"No." Derrington wiped his glossy mouth. "She kissed *me* like that."

"Yeah, right." Massie did her best to sound playful. "When?"

"After I saved a goal against the Prairie Dogs last season. It got us to the finals. And she practically jumped me."

"Puh-lease."

Derrington held up his palm. "I swear. But I didn't like it. Her lips were too puffy. They felt like a butt."

A week's worth of anxiety left Massie's body in a single sigh.

"Has she ever been in your bedroom?"

"You *are* jealous!" Derrington jumped on the pedals.

"Am nawt." Massie wrapped her arms around his waist and they started to move.

She wanted to ask him about his bedroom again, but decided to wait. All the answers she needed were minutes away.

WESTCHESTER, NY
DERRINGTON'S HOUSE
Wednesday, April 7th
4:44 P.M.

Like Derrington, his house had a style all its own. Amid a
street of old stone mansions, wrought-iron fences and foreboding
trees, "Terra Domus" was an ultramodern cube of metal
and glass.

"Hullo?" Derrington opened the red side door and stepped
into a spacious stainless-steel kitchen. It smelled like a nauseating
combination of meat sauce and lemon Pledge.

"Anyone home?"

Massie hoped no one would answer. With plans to meet
her friends at the sandwich shop in less than an hour, she
didn't have time for ah-nnoyingly polite parent banter.

"Hu-lloooo?"

"Yes, yes," answered a woman in a thick Filipino accent,
dragging a Swiffer.

"Hey, Mini. Is my mom home?"

Mini shook her head, swinging her long black hair, Pantene
style. "Six o'clock. Who's this?"

"Oh, this is my, uh, my Block." Derrington took off his
blazer and tossed it on the glass breakfast table by the port-
hole window. "Block, this is Mini."

Massie's palms tickled like she was squeezing a vibrat-
ing cell phone. The key was here. It was obvious. Skye's

poem had said she loved "all things mini." And standing before her *was* Mini. She had great hair, a knack for cleaning, and was easily a size two. What wasn't to *love*? Pure jubilation nearly allowed Massie to overlook the fact that this meant Skye had been in Derrington's room. Possibly *on* his bed. Insecurity churned inside her stomach like a curdled latte, but she did her best to remain composed. There'd be plenty of time to obsess over Skye and Derrington's relationship once the key was dangling around her neck. Puh-lenty.

"Nice to meet you, Mini." She smiled sweetly.

The cleaning woman propped the Swiffer against the shiny silver Sub-Zero fridge, then rubbed the already gleaming marble countertop with a paper towel.

"How 'bout a tour?"

"Let's go."

Derrington led Massie through a sun-drenched dining room, past a stone table with chairs made of deer antlers. A long corridor lined with splattered canvases and paintings of Campbell's Soup cans and melted clocks led to two spiral staircases.

"Let's start in the basement." Derrington gripped the cold metal banister. "It's soundproof, so I can blast video games while my brother plays the drums. Sometimes he tries to play to the beat of the game and I—"

"What about your bedroom?"

Derrington stopped.

Suddenly, Mini was beside them, dusting a marble chest

that, according to the bronze nameplate bolted to its base, had been named *A Bust*.

"You should see our new pool table. It's covered with red felt instead of green."

"I wanna see your room." Massie was all too aware of Mini and didn't want to sound like a sleaze. "To get decorating ideas for my brother."

"You don't have a brother."

"I know, but adopting is so in right now and my birthday is coming up. I already have a puppy and a horse so—"

"Um, it's really cold up there," Derrington mumbled. "The heat is broken."

Mini dusted harder.

"That's okay, I just wanna look around."

"But my mom doesn't allow guests upstairs."

Mini snickered.

"She's not home," Massie murmured, hoping her words might somehow slip by Mini undetected.

"Can't we just hang in the basement?"

Massie wondered if Skye had encountered this much trouble getting in.

Mini straightened an already straight Jonathan Adler floor vase. "Why do all females want to see inside Derrick's room?"

Massie practically exploded like a rattled can of Diet Coke. "*What* females? I'm going up." She raced to the second staircase.

"Wait, you can't!" Derrington chased after her. "Block, stop!"

"What are you so afraid of?" Massie rounded the cork-screw staircase, trying her best to fight the dizziness. "Are you hiding *Playboy*s in there?"

"No." He reddened.

"What about pictures of Skye?"

"What? No!"

Massie stopped three steps short of the landing. "Then what is it?" she asked sweetly, leaning in to kiss him.

Derrington closed his eyes.

Massie ran.

"Wait!" Derrington reached for her ankles.

But it was too late.

She pushed open the red steel door and—

"Eh. Ma. Gawd!"

Derrington chuckled nervously as they stood under his doorframe.

"I tried to stop you."

Massie buried her nose in the crook of her elbow. "What is that *smell*?" Her eyes rolled over a greasy pizza box, a clear bowl of soggy Cookie Crisp cereal, half a moldy sesame bagel, soggy green bath towels, and a heap of sweaty soccer clothes. The sisal rug added an essence of hay to the decomposing-seal-on-a-humid-day stench brought on by everything else. Massie dug inside her white leather bag, grabbed her Chanel No. 5, and sprinkled it around the room like holy water.

"The rest of your house is so clean. I don't—"

"My bed's not so bad."

The carved tin headboard illustrated some Greek myth about angry waves, windblown clouds, and teetering sailboats. His blue comforter was littered with comic books and old sports sections from the *New York Times*. The desk, which had the same carvings as the headboard, was cluttered with stacks of CDs and DVDs that loomed over his computer like prison watchtowers. Smudged press clippings on the 2006 World Cup covered every square inch of wall.

Did it look this way for Skye?

"Do you hate me now?" Derrington slid his arms around Massie's waist.

"'Course nawt." She slapped his hands away from her clean clothes. "But why don't I help you tidy?"

"You don't have—"

"Puh-lease." She slid her fingers under his mattress. "I *want* to. Grab the other side and on the count of three we'll slide this off the bed."

"Why?"

"Because we're going to bury all your . . . *stuff*."

"Block?" Derrington beamed. "I like your style."

An hour ago, those words would have filled her with frothy warm Jacuzzi bubbles. But now, after seeing—and *smelling*—his unsanitary living conditions, they slid off her like oily soap scum. The sooner she got the key, the faster she'd be outside, where she could breathe without dry heaving.

"Ready? One . . . two . . . three." Massie pushed, Derrington pulled, and a second later she was staring at a dusty box spring—a *keyless* dusty box spring.

Derrington tossed a handful of X-Men comics where the key *should* have been, and an angry dirt cloud, similar to the one on his headboard, emerged.

"Ehmagawd, what time is it?"

"Five-fifteen."

"I'm late. I have to go." Massie leaped over a tangle of action figures brought to justice in a web of vegetable lo mein.

"Want a ride?"

"No, that's okay, I'll call Isaac."

"Thought you were conserving."

"We are. But this is an emergency."

Massie raced down the stairs and back through the smell of meat sauce and lemon Pledge, which suddenly didn't seem so bad.

CURRENT STATE OF THE UNION	
IN	**OUT**
Mini's broom	Derrington's room
Derrington smells like butt.	Derrington wiggles his butt.
Dissing Derrington	Kissing Derrington

"Puh-lease tell me someone found it." Massie weaved through the 1950s-diner-style tables and sat on the edge of the horseshoe-shaped booth. Her amber eyes were vacant and sad, like she'd just lost something special, something more than the key.

Holding up two fingers, Massie let Lysa, the waitress, know she wanted her usual—a single scoop of tuna on plain wheat toast.

"Anyone?" she tried again.

"Nope." They shook their heads.

Massie unfolded her master list and put a purple slash of Glossip Girl Blueberry Pie through the names Jake Shapiro, Derrington, Josh Hotz, Tiny Nathan, and Ezra Rosenberg.

"I did find *this*." Dylan placed a ceramic mold of a buck-toothed mouth on the table. "Ew!" Alicia squealed. "Didn't we see that at the Museum of Natural History?"

"Not unless Jake Shapiro donated it." Dylan pushed back the bell sleeves on her turquoise tunic. "His father made it before his first orthodontist appointment. This was him *before* the braces."

"And you stole it?" Claire lowered her sunglasses to get a better look.

"I *had* to."

"Well, unless it unlocks that room, I'm not interested." Massie slouched.

"I bet it could." Claire giggled. "Check out that incisor."

Everyone burst out laughing, making Claire's teeth chatter. It was her body's way of releasing joy—like sweating, but for emotions. She loved how the Pretty Committee was working toward a common goal and that the goal wasn't "let's humiliate Claire." For once, they were all on the same side.

"In case anyone wants to know, Josh's room was creepy clean." Alicia licked raspberry fro yo off her spoon. "Even for a girl."

"Derrington's was creepy-dirty." Massie dipped a paper napkin in her water glass and scrubbed her hands. "He's so dead to me."

Claire stopped chattering. "Just like *that*?"

"Yup." Massie threw the soaked napkin on the table, where it landed with a soggy splat. "The bedroom is the window to the soul, Kuh-laire, and his soul smells like kitty litter."

"Ehmagawd!" Alicia grabbed Massie's wet palm. "Josh's soul smells like Mr. Clean. Let's be single together!"

"What about the double-date movie I was planning?" Claire asked, not entirely believing that Massie could change her mind about Derrington so quickly.

"Unplan it."

"Will someone puh-lease tell me a sad story?" Dylan

shoveled a pile of ketchup-covered macaroni salad in her mouth. "I *need* to lose my appetite."

Fire returned to Massie's amber eyes. "Here's one. If we don't get that key, some alt.com loser friend of Layne's will be the new alpha. Imagine being dominated by a group of girls who look like Kuh-laire does right now. By choice!"

Claire opened her mouth, ready to remind everyone that she was doing this for a movie. But Massie cut her off.

"Take off the hat and glasses," she said to Claire.

"No," Claire snapped. She was not going to be made a—

"They're mine, remember?" Massie held out her hand and wiggled her fingers. "Either take them off for a second or give them back for good."

Stone-faced, Claire removed her disguise and stared at the mini jukebox on the wall.

"Do you want eye-bangs to be in next year?"

Everyone shook their heads.

"Well, they will be if the alt.coms find that key. To them, a good wax is a tall black candle."

Alicia shuddered.

"Or the school could be run by Duh-livia Ryan." Massie crossed her eyes and poked her tongue through her teeth like an electroshock-therapy patient.

Dylan squirted another dollop of ketchup on her noodles. "I said a sad story, not a scary one." She popped a forkful of macaroni in her mouth.

Claire bit into her Say Cheese wrap. An orange glob of

cheddar oozed out, stretching toward the waxed paper, reminding her of Cam's grape gum. Ahhhh, Cam . . . with his adorable green eye and blue eye . . . his Drakkar Noir–drenched neck . . . his beat-up leather jacket . . . his—

Her cell phone buzzed.

She put her sandwich down. It was another text message from Miles.

Runaways are thin.

Freaked out by his timing and suspicious that he might be spying, Claire reluctantly hooked her finger around the gooey cheese and yanked it out.

"*C* to the *L* to the *A* to the *I* to the *R U* kidding me?" someone shouted from the front of the restaurant. "What are you *doing* here?"

"Layne?"

Claire put on her glasses.

"Here comes our new alpha," Massie snipped, "dressed in yellow low tops, pink-and-orange-striped kneesocks, denim cutoffs, and a tuxedo blazer."

Everyone snickered.

"What are *you* doing here?" Claire asked.

"He's depressed." She pointed to the takeout counter, where her brother, Chris, was lightly kicking the base of a stool.

His signature scruffy brown hair was messed to perfection. But torn jeans and a ripped black tee were an unflattering look for the otherwise preppy all-American.

"From J. Crew to Mötley Crüe," Massie muttered, obviously shocked by the sudden transformation in her old crush.

"Point."

Layne leaned closer and quickly explained. "Fawn dumpedhim. She said he spends too muchtimewithhishorse. So she spreadarumor that heputswigsonTrickyandpretends she'shisgirlfriend. Everyoneatschoolhasbeencallinghimthe HorseWhisperer and he's depressed. We're here to get his favorite meal. Number 27. The Phillycheesesteakwrap."

Claire's mouth watered.

"Ohhh, I love his horse, Tricky." Massie gathered her hair and tossed it to one side of her neck. "How could she dump him for wanting to be with her? If I don't visit my horse every week, I get—"

"Ehmagawd, didn't you used to have a crush on Chris?" Dylan asked.

"Ouch!"

Obviously, Massie had kicked her under the table with her riding boots.

"Oww-ch!"

Twice.

"Wait! Now you're both available," Kristen added. "And now that you're done with Derrington—"

"You're done with Derrington?" Layne asked.

"Hold awn," Alicia whined. "I thought we were gonna be single together."

"We are." Silently Massie urged Alicia to shut up.

"Anyway, my brother isn't available to date," said Layne. "My mom thinks he should stay single for a year." She glanced at Chris, who was reading the family's order off his hand. "It takes the wound that long to close."

"Her mom's a psychologist," Claire felt the need to explain.

"Sounds like a smart woman." Massie fake-smiled. "Now about *you*." She tapped the open space on the edge of the padded red booth. "Sit. Let's catch up."

Layne stood.

Claire took a bite of her dry, cheeseless turkey wrap and did her best to swallow.

"So?" Massie squinted as if trying to read Layne's thoughts.

"So."

"So, deliver any more balloons lately?"

"Maybe."

"Maybe?"

"Maybe."

They locked eyes. Finally, Layne broke the silence.

"Why are you so interested?"

"No reason."

"Really?"

"Really."

"Hmmmm." Layne stroked her chin.

"Hmmmm." Massie squinted.

Chris appeared behind Layne carrying two brown bags in his arms.

"Hey, Chris." Claire smiled kindly.

"Hey."

"How's tricks?" Dylan asked.

"Very funny!" He stormed off, bashing into one of those we're-so-in-love-we-can't-stop-giggling-and-kissing high school couples on his way out.

"Nice one!" Layne chased after him.

"What?" Dylan's cheeks reddened. "What'd I say?"

"His horse is named Tricky." Massie fought a smile. "He thought you were making fun of him."

Alicia and Kristen giggled.

"Oh no, I feel terrible." Dylan pushed her plate aside.

After a long pause she beamed.

"Hey, look! I feel terrible!" She pushed her plate even farther away to prove her point. "If I can stay depressed for a few days, I'll lose two pounds by Friday. Then I can wear my skinny jeans to Cam's."

Claire's stomach dipped when she heard his name.

"No," Alicia whined. "I was going to wear *my* skinny jeans."

It dipped again at thought of her friends wearing skinny jeans to his house. Then it dipped a third time because Claire knew she wouldn't be there.

She pinched the hardening gob of discarded cheddar off the waxed paper and dropped it in her mouth. Unfortunately for Miles, depression had the opposite effect on her.

┌───┐
│   │
│   OCTAVIAN COUNTRY DAY SCHOOL   │
│   THE SOCCER FIELD   │
│   Friday, April 9th   │
│   4:22 P.M.   │
│   │
└───┘

After a tiring week at school and endless key hunting, the last place Massie wanted to be on Friday afternoon was on a soccer field doing jumping jacks with a team of jumping-jack-loving girls in loose boy shorts and ill-fitting yellow tees.

"This warm-up isn't working." Alicia rubbed her bare arms. "I'm freezing. It's a day for denim and cashmere, nawt cotton."

"Ah-greed," Dylan panted. "If I get sick, can we get your dad to sue the coach?"

"Given."

"Claire's so lucky," Massie huffed.

"Why? 'Cause she has those eyebrows to keep her warm?" Alicia snickered.

"And auditions to get her out of practice?" Dylan offered.

"All of the above." Massie sighed, wondering how Claire could abandon the Pretty Committee—during key season— for a director who wanted her to look like a "before" picture.

Puuuuuuurp. Purrrrrrp.

Instantly, the Sirens stopped jumping.

Coach Davis cupped her hands around her mouth and shouted, "I want everyone dribbling!"

Dylan turned to Massie and Alicia, a string of saliva dangling off her bottom lip. "How's that?"

The entire team tittered, except for Kristen, who crouched to tie her already tied laces.

"E-nuff!" The coach blew her whistle an inch away from Dylan's wet lips. "Kori!" she yelled. "How 'bout those balls?"

"She said *balls*," Dylan whisper-snickered.

Massie and Alicia burst out laughing.

Despite her swollen knee, Kori was dragging the yellow mesh bag across the field. "Coming!"

The sight of her limping and tugging made the girls laugh even harder.

"What's so funny?" snapped the coach.

"Nothing." Dylan giggled. "It's just that you said—" She cracked up all over again.

PUUURRRRPPP!

"You three! Drop and give me seventy-five sit-ups."

Coach Davis hurried toward center field, the bottoms of her coral Juicy sweat suit dragging across the grass. "The rest of you, over here!"

Massie, Alicia, and Dylan lowered themselves onto the cold field.

"Who wears peach in April?" Alicia said once they were alone.

"Your dad." Dylan giggled.

"Very funny." Alicia ripped a handful of grass out of the ground and whipped it at Dylan's face.

Massie rolled her eyes, temporarily hating her friends for having fun when they should be obsessing over the key.

After two crunches and a quick check to make sure the coach wasn't looking, she pulled her list of boys' names from her white kneesock and rested it against her thighs.

"I should only have to do fifty of these," Alicia huffed, barely lifting her shoulders off the grass. "My boobs are like weights."

Dylan cracked up. "So is my hair."

"Let's go over this one more time." Massie curled toward the list.

"We have," Alicia whined. "Like nine *hundred* times."

Massie stopped midcrunch to glare at her.

"Sorry."

"Quit talking!" Kori shouted from the bench.

"Quit breathing!" Massie shouted back. "Dylan, you checked Cody, Luis, and Billy, right?"

"Right." Dylan lifted her neck, then lowered it. "The only thing I found was a stack of Sudoku mags under Luis's mattress and an Ashlee Simpson CD under Billy's."

Massie slid the tube of Glossip Girl Blueberry Pie out from her other sock and drew a purple *X* through their names.

"Leesh? What about Greer, Lowell, Andy, Oliver, and Liam?"

"No, no, no, no, and no. But FYI, Lowell sleeps in a tent on an air mattress. He invited me to his camping birthday party. He's gonna try and set the record for number of beetles caught in an empty peanut-butter jar."

Alicia and Dylan looked at Massie, expecting her to say

something clever about Lowell's LBR-ness, but she was too stressed to bother.

Glossy purple *X*s through Geoff, P.J., and Lee's names were cruel reminders that none of Kristen's guys had panned out either. If Harris Fisher didn't have the key, Massie would have to reanalyze Skye's poem, restrategize the plan, and redeploy her troops. It could take days, and someone else could win. And before they knew it, they'd be begging for invitations to Lowell's beetle birthday party.

In the parking lot, an old Eminem song blasted from a car's speakers, turning everyone's attention to a dirty black Mustang.

"Ehmagawd, it's Harris Fisher." Alicia propped herself up on her elbows. "I think my crush on him is back."

"You're not the only one." Dylan pointed at the two girls wearing similar beige trench coats, running toward his car.

"Since when are Kaya and Penelope all buddy-buddy with Harris Fisher?"

"They think he has the key," Massie assumed.

"They must have the other two CD-ROMs," Dylan concluded.

Without a single word, Massie jumped to her feet and took off toward the Mustang. "Come awn!"

"Wait!" Dylan rolled onto her side, then pushed herself up.

"Yeah, wait!" Alicia speed-walked behind them.

Puuuurp. Puuuurp.

"Stop!" Coach Davis waved her toned arms like she was hailing a cab. "Now!"

Massie froze.

The coach jogged to meet them by the fence, eyeing two trails of uprooted grass left behind in Alicia's wake.

"What happened to the field?" she gasped.

Alicia checked the bottoms of her shoes like someone who'd just stepped in dog poo. The metal spikes were covered in mud and weeds.

"Miss Rivera, you're wearing cleats, not cross-country skis. The idea is to lift them when you run."

"Huh?"

The coach's green eyes softened and the crease in her forehead smoothed. "Girls." She forced a grin. "Do you care about your school?"

While nodding, Massie snuck a peek at the parking lot. Kaya and Penelope were making small circles with their fists, gesturing for Harris to roll down his window.

"Do you care about the OCD Sirens?"

They nodded again.

"And are you aware that we have a chance to make it to the finals?"

"Uh-huh," Massie managed as the competition poked their heads in the open window.

"Then please, I'm begging you. . . ." The coach put her hands together in prayer position, obviously about to plead for their undying cooperation and dedication.

Alicia rolled her eyes. Dylan twirled her hair. Massie fought the urge to charge Kaya and Penelope.

"Please, please, please," the coach continued, "will you *please* quit the team?"

"*What*?" they all said.

"I'm sorry if this hurts your feelings. It can be our secret. In fact, I'll tell Principal Burns you injured your ankles from overexertion." She zipped her lip and threw away the key. "Just *please* don't play Sunday, and stop coming to practice."

"Seriously?" Alicia beamed.

Coach placed a reassuring hand on her shoulder. "Seriously."

"Done." Massie pulled her friends by the arms and dragged them off the field. "Tell Kristen we'll call her later."

The coach responded with a huge smile and a thumbs-up.

"Don't you think we should change outfits first?" Alicia freed herself from Massie's grip. "We can't talk to Harris like *this*." She pinched her baggy Sirens uniform.

While walking, Massie tied a knot on either side of her shirt, instantly tightening it. She rolled down the elastic waistband on the shorts and pulled off her socks. Wrapping one around her left wrist, she stuffed the other through the mesh fence on her way out.

Dylan and Alicia did the same.

Scooting Kaya and Penelope aside, Massie stuck her head in the car's open window. "Hey, Harris. I'm Massie, Cam's friend."

It took all of Massie's strength to look at him straight on because a) his green eyes were piercing, and b) Kaya was tugging at her shirt.

"What brings you to OCD?" she eked out.

"Pickin' up my brother and his friends after practice." He cocked his head and squinted, probably wondering why girls had surrounded his car like he was Nick Lachey.

"Perf!"

Massie opened the door and slid across the backseat. Alicia and Dylan jammed in beside her.

"Wait a minute." Penelope adjusted her skinny double-wire headband. "We were here first."

"Back off!" Massie hit the automatic lock. She blew a kiss to Kaya and Penelope as they skulked off toward the bike rack.

Harris turned. "What's going on?" He smiled, showing amusement, not concern. His teeth were so white and his eyes so green, Massie had to focus on the distressed collar of his brown leather jacket, to minimize the glare.

"Cam invited us over after practice, so we thought we'd ride with you because my driver is sick. Is that okay?"

Quickly she texted Isaac with the change of plans.

"Sure." He turned up the stereo, blasting the Eminem song all over again.

Dylan shouted the lyrics while Harris bobbed to the beat.

You better lose yourself in the music, the moment—

"So how was the visit with your uncle?" Massie shouted toward the front seat, hoping conversation might make Harris lower the music.

"What uncle?" he shouted back.

"The uncle who visited you on Tuesday."

"I don't have an uncle."

Massie shot Alicia a confused glance.

"Does Cam?" Alicia tried.

Dylan burst out laughing, but to Massie, the situation was far from funny.

"Why would Claire lie to me?" she mumbled.

"Maybe she didn't want us at Cam's without her," Alicia said.

"Why would we go without—?" Massie stopped, remembering that Tuesday was the night Claire had her meeting in Manhattan.

"Ehmagawd, how could she jeopardize the future of the Pretty Committee for a *boy*?"

"*I* would *never* do that," Alicia gasped.

"Me *either*," Dylan said.

Massie clenched her fist. "She is so dead to—"

"Unlock the doors." Cam pounded the roof of the car. His black hair was matted to his forehead. Both his blue eye and green eye were bright against the pink flush of his sweaty cheeks.

"What's the password?" Harris cranked the music.

One of the boys made a fart sound and everyone burst out laughing.

"Ew!" Alicia squealed. "Dylan!"

"It wasn't *me*."

Let's go! Massie wanted to scream, hell-bent on getting the key. But instead she smiled and giggled with the rest of them to avoid blowing their cover.

"Open up!" Derrington, Josh, and Cam smacked the roof, giving Harris even more of a Nick Lachey moment than the one he'd experienced earlier.

Finally, the locks clicked and the boys piled in. Cam raced to the front seat while Derrington conquered the back.

"What's up, soccer sistas?" He wiggled his butt, then dove across the girls, landing with his head on Massie's lap. There was a time where it would have been funny, even romantic. But all Massie could think of now was his crumb-covered carpet and musty towels.

Gazing up at her, eyebrows raised, mouth in a barely there pout, Derrington seemed to be silently asking Massie with kind brown eyes why she tore out of his house the other day. Guiltily, she turned her attention to the others, as if they were up to something utterly fascinating that she simply could not miss.

"Ow, get offa me," Alicia whined when Dylan mashed up against her thigh.

"It's Josh's fault, not mine."

"Yeah, right." Josh giggled, his round brown eyes crinkling.

A slapping fight broke out among Dylan, Josh, and Alicia, spreading a dry-sweat-meets-grass smell throughout the car. Harris turned up the stereo even louder and backed out of the lot.

You only get one shot, do not miss your chance to blow—

"Who's ready for some soccer lessons?" Cam asked from the front seat.

Everyone cheered.

Dylan burped.

Massie lifted her wrist to her nose and inhaled deeply. She *would* survive this loud, stinky car ride thanks to three things:

1. Determination
2. Hope
3. Chanel No. 5

WESTCHESTER, NY
THE FISHER HOUSE
Friday, April 9th
5:55 P.M.

The metal drawers on Cam's Pottery Barn locker desk were like his eyes, one green and one blue. They felt cold against Massie's bare legs. She leaned against them anyway, because they, like everything in his bedroom, were clean.

"Show us how to do that kick where you fall and score at the same time. Fans love that."

"Maybe we should go out back for that." Cam surveyed his crowded room.

Derrington was bouncing a soccer ball on his foot while Dylan slid across the hardwood floors on Cam's light blue desk chair. Alicia and Josh were perched on the edge of his bed, which doubled as a storage hutch. The bulky oak frame had six cubbyholes stacked above the headboard and overflowing with rows of folded T-shirts. Hundreds of CD booklets were neatly tacked to his navy-painted walls, their jewel cases converted into an intricate maze that twisted and turned along the wood floor in the far corner.

"I say we do it right here." Massie emphasized each word, urging Dylan and Alicia to stick to the plan. "We can use the bed as a mat."

"Ah-greed." Alicia jumped to her feet and made a show of trying to pull the mattress onto the floor.

"Good idea." Dylan raced over.

"I still think it would be better if we went outside," Cam said, while casually sliding a framed a photo of Claire off his night table and into a tiny drawer. It was a close-up of her slurping an orange gummy worm like a piece of spaghetti. The sweet shot filled Massie with bitterness. Why wasn't Claire with them? Why hadn't she called to wish them luck? And why, why weren't there any ah-dorable pictures of Massie in Derrington's room?

"Outside is so *far*," Alicia whined. "All we need is a little padding and we can stay right here." She stepped away from the bed and stood behind Josh and Dylan. "Ready? One . . . two . . . three . . . pull!"

They yanked the mattress onto the floor with a thud.

Cam checked the jewel case maze, which miraculously remained intact.

As Massie had suspected, the key wasn't there. It was time for phase two of their plan.

"Kick-fall!" Derrington took a running dive toward Dylan and gave her a leg-sweep, knocking her face-first onto the mattress.

"Not with cleats!" pleaded Cam.

"Get! Off!" Dylan laughed as she fought her way out from under Derrington. "Your pits smell like sour cream and onion chips."

Derrington lifted his arm and smeared his post-soccer practice stink in her nose.

"Ew!" Dylan squirmed frantically.

And then—"*Baaaap*"—she burped and blew it in his face.

Everyone laughed, including Derrington.

Even though the last thing Massie wanted was Derrington's sweaty BO near her T-zone, she found herself temporarily hating Dylan for flirting with him.

"Ehmagawd, did your back just crack?" Massie stood above them, showing no signs of amusement.

"What?" Dylan giggled. "No, I burp—"

"No, that *crack*." Massie winked at Alicia.

"Yeah, I heard it too."

"Oh yeah," Dylan blurted, her face suddenly becoming serious. "I think I hurt my lumbar." With a single buck she managed to throw Derrington off her. "We definitely need more padding."

"Good call." Massie perked up. "Let's get Harris's mattress and put it on top of this one."

"Heart that!" Alicia clapped. "I'll help."

"Me too." Dylan smoothed her navy-and-yellow Sirens uniform.

"Hold it!" Cam held out his palm like a crossing guard.

"Come awn!" Massie led the charge. She slammed Cam's bedroom door on her way out, paying little mind to the sound of shattering plastic that must have been the domino effect ripping through his jewel-case maze.

The girls burst into Harris's room and locked the door.

Old movie posters of guys she didn't recognize hung in what smelled like a Scotch-tape factory.

"Open up!" Cam pounded.

"Ehmagawd!" Massie gasped. "Twin beds!"

Dylan cracked her knuckles. "No problem."

Massie dashed to her side. "Ready?"

Alicia moved quickly (for Alicia) and grabbed a fistful of burgundy comforter.

"Okay," Massie grunted. "Ready . . . set . . . go!"

After four shoves, the mattress slid onto the floor.

A crumpled magazine photo of Pamela Anderson in her red *Baywatch* swimsuit stared back at them, along with three strands of brown hair and an orange Tic Tac.

"Let me in!" Cam shouted.

"We're trying—the door is stuck." Dylan jiggled the handle for effect.

"This is it." Massie raced over to the bed by the window and dropped to her knees. With an adrenaline-charged push, she flipped the second mattress without any help.

Dylan and Alicia dashed to her side.

"Ehmagawd," they all said, staring down at the white web of cotton that coated the box spring.

There, reflecting the last glimmer of golden light the day had to offer, was a shiny silver . . . dime.

WESTCHESTER, NY
THE ABELEY HOUSE
Friday, April 9th
7:12 P.M.

"Whoa! What happened?" gasped Layne when she opened her front door and saw Claire on her porch, alone in the cold, starless night. Tears streamed from beneath her over-size glasses, blazing salty trails through the beige foundation on her cheeks.

"Are you in trouble with the law?" Layne's tongue was Crystal Light purple.

Sobbing, Claire turned and waved, letting her mother know it was okay to leave.

The headlights on the Lyonses' bronze Ford Taurus lit the front of the Abeleys' redbrick house as Judi backed out of the driveway, illuminating their WOW, NICE UNDERWEAR straw doormat.

"Is it the audition?" Layne twirled one of the seven braids in her hair. "Was Bernard Sinrod mean to you? Did he beat you?" She made a move to pull off her best friend's glasses, but Claire jumped back.

"He punched you in the eye, didn't he?"

Claire shook her head no. It felt puffy and full. She sniffed back the snot bubble that grew and shrank every time she blubbered.

"Don't worry. Rejection is part of the biz." Layne placed

a well-meaning hand on Claire's shoulder, which was bare and cold thanks to the tattered black tube top Miles had suggested she wear. "Wait till your movie comes out next month. You'll be turning down more scripts than Lindsay."

It was funny getting career advice from someone in Chococat baby-doll pajamas and headgear, but Claire couldn't bring herself to smile.

"Come inside. My brother is upstairs listening to Ne-Yo's 'So Sick' on repeat. He can cry about Fawn and you can cry about not getting the part and—"

"I *did* get it." Claire sniffed. "The lawyers will be at my house tomorrow to look over the contract."

"Brava!" Layne unclipped her headgear and tossed it in the air like a graduation cap. "When do you start shooting?"

"Summer."

"Did you meet Cole Sprouse?"

"Next week, when we read the script."

"Is Bernard nice?"

"Totally." Claire sighed. "He gave me roses. My mom has them." Her vision blurred all over again and the backs of her eyes pinched.

"Then what is it?" Layne picked her headgear off the Oriental carpet and clipped it around her neck. The two spiked ends pointed straight at her jugular and gave Claire an uneasy feeling.

"It's complicated." Claire stepped into the small square receiving room, just beyond the front door. The walls on either side of her were covered in mirrors, creating the illusion of a thousand Claires. There was "friend Claire" and "actress Claire" and "Cam's Claire" and "Pretty Committee Claire" and "sister Claire" and "daughter Claire" and "student Claire" and "Orlando Claire" and "Westchester Claire." They went on and on.

Most days, each one was a part of her, making her whole. But tonight the Claires felt like strangers with different sets of plans.

Without thinking, Claire removed her sunglasses and tossed her hat onto the black lacquer table beside the Oriental screen.

Layne squinted. Her thin, light brows arched above her narrow green eyes. "Wha—?"

"Oh." Claire suddenly realized what she had done but decided to go with it. She was an actress. And with that came sacrifices. Sooner or later, everyone would have to accept it. Herself included. "I had to do this for my audition."

"Well, can you tell me why you're crying?" Layne sighed. "Or are you too *bushed*?" She tried to contain her laughter, then snorted instead.

"Sounds like you've been hanging around Massie."

"Ehmagawd, rea-lly?" Layne gushed, offering her best Pretty Committee impersonation.

Claire couldn't help smiling as she followed her one-of-a-kind friend up the ruby-red-carpeted staircase.

"So what *happened*?" Layne asked again from the top of the stairs.

Claire took a deep breath.

"I went to Cam's after the audition because everyone was going there after school to look for the—" She caught herself just in time. "Uh, to look for soccer tips. And Mrs. Fisher told me she sent Massie, Alicia, and Dylan home because they destroyed Cam's and Harris's bedrooms. When I asked to see Cam she told me I couldn't 'cause he was grounded for letting them do that to her house."

"Wow, poor Cam. I wonder why they did that." Layne kicked the blowup pit bull away from her bedroom door, ignoring the terrifying bark and growl recording that played every time someone moved it from its guard post. "And *that's* why you were crying?"

"No." Claire instinctively grabbed Layne's elbow when they entered her famous glow-in-the-dark bedroom, allowing herself to be led through the pitch-black labyrinth filled with all things luminescent: oozing lava lamps, posters of big-headed martians, and fiery-haired trolls. Finally they reached her bed, the duvet a massive canvas of neon orange, yellow, and hot pink splattered paints. Above it, the solar system in sticker form clung to her ceiling, the stars and planets shining in a radioactive shade of green.

"I was crying because when I called Massie to tell her I was on my way to her sleepover she freaked out on me."

"Why? Because you got the part and she didn't?"

"She didn't even audition."

"So, I'm sure she still expected to get the part."

Claire giggled, tickled by how well Layne had Massie figured out. "She *uninvited* me to the sleepover and kicked me out of the Pretty Committee. Forever."

"Why?"

The tears returned.

"She thinks I stood in the way of her and the—" Claire stopped. A flood of prickly heat itched her palms, reminding her how dangerously close she had come to breaking Skye's number-one rule.

"Her and the *what*?"

"Nothing."

"What?"

"Nothing!" Then Claire felt a tugging on her arm. "Layne, what are you—?"

Suddenly, she was being gagged with a glow-in-the-dark Hello Kitty scarf.

"Mmmmmmm," she called. The black room, with all its brightly colored inhabitants, made Claire feel like she had been beamed to an animated planet. "Mmmmmm!"

A blast of electronica music drowned out Claire's pleas, turning her fear into panic. Suddenly, someone plopped down beside her. The smell of artificial grape flavoring got stronger and stronger until Claire felt hot breath against her cheek.

"I know," whispered Layne.

"Mmmmm?" She grunted as loud as she could, hoping to be heard above the pulsating music. "Mmmm!"

"I know about the keyyyy," Layne whispered again.

Claire ripped the scarf off, wondering why she hadn't tried that sooner. "You do?"

Layne's hand smacked against her mouth. "Shhhhhh, she might be listening."

Claire nodded, taking Layne's hand for a ride.

"I'm going to show you something. But don't speak."

Layne turned on the lights.

A bouquet of helium balloons, each with a different message and a guy's name on them bobbed against the ceiling. They said, JOSH IS NUMBER 1, GET WELL, JAKE, and BEST WISHES, LUIS—obviously her way in to boys' houses.

So Alicia was right. Heather *had* gotten a CD-ROM, and she'd recruited Layne and Meena to help.

"Did you find any—?"

"Ouija?" Layne instantly cut her off. She reached behind her pillow and pulled out the creepy game used to contact the dead. She crossed her legs and balanced the game board on her knees. Claire wiggled into position so that the other side of the board rested on her.

The alphabet, written in sinister black font, was laid out before them. Without asking the Ouija board a question, Layne placed her fingertips on the oval slab of wood and moved it over certain letters.

Suddenly Claire understood. Layne wasn't using the board to get help from beyond. She was using it to communicate her thoughts. It was like text messaging without the technology trail.

A-N-Y-L-E-A-D-S, she spelled.

N-O-A-N-D-M-A-S-S-I-E-I-S-F-R-E-A-K-I-N-G-T-H-E-R-E-
H-A-S-T-O-B-E-S-O-M-E-O-N-E-W-E-R-E-N-O-T-T-H-I-N-K-
I-N-G-O-F

W-H-O

D-I-D-U-C-H-E-C-K-E-V-E-R-Y-O-N-E-S-K-Y-E-K-I-S-S-E-D

Layne reached for the slab.

Y-E-A-H-Y-O-U

D-O-H-E-R-S-H-E-Y-S-C-O-U-N-T

"Huh?" Claire said out loud.

H-E-R-S-H-E-Y-S-K-I-S-S-E-S

Layne snickered, then cupped her hands around her
heart-shaped mouth.

"Just kidding."

"What?" Claire asked.

Layne whispered, "She gave Chris a bag of Hershey's
Kisses last month when he drove her home."

"Seriously?" Claire asked at full volume.

"Shhhhh!" Layne fanned her mouth like she'd just taken
a bite of burning-hot pizza. "Unless Skye works for the CIA
and you're wanted, the room is probably safe."

Layne giggled, then tossed the Ouija board on the floor.

"Skye gives Hershey's Kisses to every guy who gives her
a ride. It's her thing."

"Did you check—?" Claire stiffened with regret.

A subtle twitch on the side of Layne's jaw told Claire
they were thinking the same thing.

"Outta my way." Layne rolled off the bed, commando
style, and bolted out of her bedroom door.

Claire raced after her, thinking more about Massie than the key. This was her chance to redeem herself in the eyes of the Pretty Committee . . . for life.

In an act of total desperation, she shoved Layne into a freaky decorative totem pole outside the bathroom and squeezed past her.

The muffled sound of Ne-Yo told Claire that Chris's bedroom was at the end of the short hall. Slipping on the narrow Oriental rug, she quickly regained her balance and reached for the brass doorknob like it was a life preserver. Layne was right behind her, giggle-panting.

Claire jiggled the handle.

It was locked.

"Chris, let me in, code red!" Layne pounded.

Claire joined in. She even shouted, "Code red," figuring it would sound redder if two people were screaming it.

"Chill." Chris let them in, then dove back onto his bed and spooned a navy quilted throw pillow.

"Sorry to bother you—"

"Whoa, who's the dude?" he asked, lifting his head.

"It's me. Claire." She covered her eyebrows and smiled shyly. "It's for a movie."

"Whatever." He tossed a stuffed deer at the ceiling, then caught it. Then did it again. And again. And again.

"What are you doing to Lil' Fawn?" Layne asked, as if the doe-eyed Gund were alive.

"It's not Lil' Fawn anymore," he mumbled. "It's just a stupid deer." He whipped it across the room, knocking over the mini-cologne menagerie on his black dresser. The bottles scattered onto the hardwood floor, but he didn't seem to notice.

Feeling sorry for him, Claire dropped to her knees and started gathering them. A burgundy Clarins bottle shot toward the wall covered in pictures of his friends from boarding school and Tricky, his beloved black horse. A little bottle of Fahrenheit Summer landed near a heap of dirty jeans and torn T-shirts by the closet, and the Rive Gauche lay beneath his glass desk, near the silver mesh trash can. Inside was a heap of torn photographs of a pretty blonde with a wide toothy smile. And suddenly Claire knew.

Chris's bedroom *was* Skye's poem. The cologne samples meant he was a mini lover, and there was no question how he felt about "all creatures, big and small," especially horses. And ever since Fawn had dumped him, his clothes had been stained, ripped, or both, something even Claire knew was "*Glamour*-don't" style.

"Maybe you should get off the bed and get some fresh air." Claire tried her best to sound constructive.

Chris rolled onto his side.

"What was the code red?" he mumbled.

"Um, nothing. We were just worried about you." Layne twirled her horse-locket necklace around her stained index finger.

Claire scanned the room, desperate for inspiration. She found it in the half-empty bottle of Mike's Hard Lemonade beside his Dell. After a quick pantomime, where she demonstrated throwing the drink on Chris, Claire handed it to Layne. They both bit their lower lips, which trembled with a combination of guilt and giggles.

And then . . .

"Ah-ah-ah-choooo!" Layne dumped the leftover lemonade on Chris's neck.

"What the?!" He jumped to his feet.

"Claire, why do you always push me when I sneeze?"

"Um, s-sorry, Chris," was all she could think to say.

"Sorry. We'll change your sheets while you clean up," Layne insisted.

"*Girls*, man!" Chris grumbled as he stormed off to the bathroom. "I am so going back to boarding school."

"Help me lift." Layne squatted.

Without hesitation, Claire slid her hands into position. "Ready? One . . . two . . . three . . ."

With a single hoist, they flipped the mattress off the bed. And there it was.

Massie pulled the cap off her purple Sharpie mini. "Yes, I'm calling from the Board of Health. Did you ever make out with Skye Hamilton?" She sat cross-legged in the middle of her purple down-filled duvet. Alicia, Dylan, and Kristen faced her, like preschool kids during story time.

"I wish," snickered Deron McEvoy before hanging up.

"Ugh!" She crossed another name off her list. "Who's next?"

"Jack Rubell," Alicia read.

While Massie dialed, Alicia wiggled out of her nylon soccer shorts and slipped into a pair of buttery soft black Splendid sweats.

"Yes, um, I'm calling from the Board of Health. Did you ever make out with Skye Hamilton?" She rolled her eyes, already knowing the answer. It was the same one eleven other guys had already given.

"No." he paused. "Wait. Sarah, if this is you, I'm telling Dad."

"Double ugh!" Massie whipped her phone across the room. It landed on one of her fluffy ivory sheepskin area rugs.

"I'll get it this time." Kristen jumped off the bed and hurried to the rescue.

Massie buried her head in her hands.

One of the girls placed a comforting hand on her curved shoulder while another finger-combed her hair. Bean licked her elbow.

"How about some nice chamomile tea?" Kristen offered, handing her back the phone. "It's very soothing."

"Ew!" Massie glared at Kristen through the spaces between her fingers. "Chamomile sounds like Cam. And Cam reminds me of Mrs. Fisher kicking us out of her house for making a mess, and making a mess reminds me of the key, and the key reminds me of—"

"Okay, forget it!"

"Sorry." She sighed. "But we're down to our last guy and something tells me Skye did not kiss Shawn O'Hare."

"You mean Shawn O'Harelip?" Dylan made a distorted kissy face.

Kristen cackled.

Lifting her Motorola, Massie looked deep into the eyelike camera lens and warned, "Bring me luck, or I'm getting a Samsung." After a deep, cleansing breath, she dialed the last eleven digits on her list of potential key keepers.

"Hi, Shawn? Um, I'm calling from the Board of Health. Did you ever make out with Skye Hamilton?"

Beep. Beep.

Call waiting interrupted before he could answer.

"Well, did you?" Massie hurried him along.

"Uhhh, can you call back after my supper?"

Beep. Beep.

"Whatevs." Massie jammed her thumb into the red END button, then quickly checked her screen. It flashed **UNKNOWN CALLER**.

"Bet it's Claire, begging for forgiveness because of the whole uncle lie." Alicia rubbed Crabtree & Evelyn sesame oil on her cuticles.

"I still can't believe she did that," Dylan huffed.

Kristen shook her head in disbelief. "Me either."

Tightening the sash on her white chenille robe, Massie stood. It was against her policy to answer UCs. And it was double against her policy to answer if it was Claire. But what if it was a lead? She hit speaker and the girls pressed an ear against her Razr.

"Hullo?"

"I. Have. What. You. Want," said a computerized voice.

Everyone's eyes widened, silently questioning Massie on her next move.

"Um, can I get your number? I'll call you right back from a landline. My reception is—"

"No. Landline. Talk. Now."

"What do you want?"

"We. Have. Demands. Do. What. We. Say. And. We. Will. Give. You. The. Key."

"Reveal your identity or I'm hanging up."

Alicia gasped.

Massie knew her approach was risky, but what if Skye was testing her? The rules clearly stated she was not to discuss this with *anyone*. So obviously the way to play this was to act dumb. Dumb and safe. Unless, of course, this was a legitimate caller who really had the key. And if it was, the last thing Massie wanted to do was drive this person toward the competition by not cooperating.

"Ugh, just tell me who you are," she snapped.

"Do. What. We. Say."

"Re-veal."

Alicia bit her fist, Kristen covered her mouth, and Dylan stuffed a cube of Blue Razzberry Bubble Yum in her mouth.

"Do—"

"Reveal," Massie interrupted.

"Good. Bye."

The line went dead.

Massie whipped the sweaty phone onto her bed. Dylan raced to retrieve it.

"Ehmagawd." Alicia flapped her hands like a baby bird trying to take flight. "Now what? What if they offer it to someone else?"

Taking her phone back, Massie scrolled through her received-calls log. Her hand quaked with a mix of frustration and fear. The only thing worse than losing was being made a fool of, and at the moment, she was at risk for both. She highlighted **UNKNOWN CALLER** and pressed send with such force her thumb turned white. But the phone wouldn't make the call.

"Ugh!" She whipped it across the room and flopped down on her bed, trying to figure out her next move.

And then, as if by magic, her cell rang.

"Get that!" Massie called.

Kristen darted across the hardwood floor like she was sprinting for soccer drills and pulled the Motorola out from under Massie's purple-faux-fur-covered desk chair. "It's the UC."

"Hurry." Massie leaped off the bed and raced to meet her in the middle of the room. Without hesitation, she flipped open the phone and lifted it to her ear. "Hullo?"

A shuffling sound, like someone rubbing their cheek against the speaker, was all she heard.

"Hul-lo?" Massie pleaded again, loudly.

"What is that?" someone on the other end whisper-shouted. "Oh no! Your butt just dialed Massie. *Stand up!"*

"Kuh-laire, is that you?"

"Quick, press end!"

"I did, nothing happened. . . ."

"Shhh, she can hear us. Say something."

"Hell. O," said a girl in a robot voice.

Massie rolled her eyes. "Layne?"

The line went dead.

"Busted!" Alicia punched the air.

Dylan and Kristen burst out laughing. They turned their palms to Massie, who pushed them aside and belly-flopped onto her bed.

"Do you really think *they* found it?"

"Puh-lease!" Dylan dove beside her, sending puffy duvet waves across the bed. "Claire's just trying to pay us back for kicking her out of the Pretty Committee."

"Point!" Alicia wiggled across the queen-size mattress and joined them.

"If they found it, why wouldn't they keep it?" Dylan asked.

"Because they know I'll make their lives miserable," Massie mumbled into a pink satin throw pillow.

"What now?" Kristen sat beside her.

"This." Massie hit last call received. Someone picked up after the first ring.

"Do you have the key or nawt?"

After some fumbling and frantic whisper-panicking, Layne said, "Yes."

"Where did you find it?"

"Under Chris Abeley's bed," Claire chimed in.

"Ehmagawd, Kuh-laire?" Massie felt sick to her stomach. "You're involved in *this*?"

"Yup," she replied proudly.

"Well, as the head of the Pretty Committee, I insist you hand it over." Massie wished she could text her hand to Claire's phone and smack her. "If you don't, you will be charged with treason."

"You kicked me out, remember?" Claire sounded like she was sticking out her tongue. "Your rules don't apply to me."

Massie temporarily hated Claire for being right.

"Well, I want proof."

Layne scraped the key against the phone.

"You should have seen his bedroom," Claire boasted. "It *was* the poem."

She told them about the mini-cologne bottles, the "*Glamour*-don't" clothes, his love of horses, and, most important, the Hershey's Kisses.

"*No way!*" Massie remembered Liam crumpling up the silver foil and tossing it onto Skye's driveway. How could she have missed that? It had been right in front of her face.

"Um, can you hold on a minute?" Massie covered the phone and turned to Alicia. "Why didn't you put Chris Abeley's name on the list?"

"Uh, I—"

Then she turned to Kristen. "Why didn't you tell me Skye was into Hershey's?"

"How was I sup—?"

"And Dylan, I can't believe you let Claire lie to us about Cam's uncle."

"I didn't know—"

"Kuh-laire, I insist you give me the key ay-sap."

"We will." Layne continued scraping. "Once you meet our demands."

Alicia, Kristen, and Dylan cheered silently. But Massie knew it wasn't going to be that easy.

"Kuh-laire, this is crazy," Massie hissed. "Whose side are you on?"

"The side of justice." Claire's voice was steady and confident. "Like she said, we have demands."

"Fine." Massie rolled her eyes. "What do you want?"

"We have a list," Layne grumbled. "Where can we meet?"

"E-mail it," Massie snapped.

"Where? Can? We? *Meet?*" Layne sounded like a frustrated parent who was not going to ask again.

"My house," Alicia offered. "Dad's home office has a huge conference table, and I know where he keeps his legal pads. Everyone can have one."

"Fine," Massie said firmly, hoping to regain some control. "One-thirty at the Riveras'."

"Done," said Dylan.

"Done," said Kristen.

"And done," said Alicia.

Claire whispered to Layne, something about movie contracts and lawyers.

"How's Sunday?" Layne asked, sounding slightly perturbed.

"Nope, no good," Massie insisted.

The line went dead.

"Ehmagawd, did they seriously hang up again?" Alicia's brown eyes were wide with disbelief.

This time Massie dialed Claire.

"Hey," she answered, a trace of shame in her voice.

"Are you a pyromaniac?"

"No, why?" Claire sounded confused.

Alicia, Kristen, and Dylan covered their mouths in anticipation.

"'Cause you're playing with *fire*!"

"I-I'm not," Claire stammered. "It's just that I can't do it tomorrow. I have a meeting with some lawyers." She paused, obviously waiting for someone to ask why. But Massie wasn't about to give her the satisfaction.

Finally, she volunteered, "I got the part."

A cashmere-coated lump formed in the back of Massie's throat. She knew she should say something, to avoid seeming upset. But she couldn't. The cashmere was spreading into her brain, smothering all thoughts, words, and I'm-so-happy-for-you sounds.

"Well, if you're moving to Hollywood, you won't care *when* we meet," Alicia said.

Massie winked, indicating a nice save.

"We want Sunday." Layne scraped the key against the phone.

"Hmmm." Massie sighed dreamily.

"What?" Layne and Claire asked at the same time.

"I was just wondering." Massie stood at her bay window, like a queen looking at out her kingdom. "What do you think Skye would do if she knew you were bargaining with her key? I mean, isn't this supposed to be secretive?"

Alicia clapped silently, while Dylan and Kristen urged Massie along with two, enthusiastic, thumbs-up.

"If I were her, and you betrayed me like that," Massie addressed the forest of oak trees in her backyard, "I'd assign someone to make your eighth-grade life feel like death. Someone, like, oh, I dunno . . . *me!*"

"Fine," Layne blurted. "Alicia's tomorrow at one-thirty."

"What?" Claire whined. "You can't—"

Once again, the line went dead. This time it was Massie who hung up.

She collapsed on the purple-pillow-covered ledge beneath her window, burying her face again. The future of the Pretty Committee was in the Crystal Light–stained hands of Layne Abeley and Miss Keds "R" Us, Claire Lyons. "What did I do to deserve this?"

"Don't worry, we'll get the key." Alicia crouched and put her arm around Massie. "I've gone to court with my dad a million times. I know how to negotiate."

"What if she wants us to take her shopping at second-hand stores or—?"

"Relax." Alicia grabbed Massie's frigid hand and looked her in the eye. "Remember that famous plastic-surgery case last summer?"

Massie shook her head no, even though she did. It was the point that escaped her.

"Was that the one where that cocktail waitress wanted a body like Jessica Simpson's?" Kristen giggled.

Alicia nodded.

"Oh, I remember that one." Dylan finally peeled off her soccer uniform and slipped into one of Mr. Block's old XL Brooks Brothers shirts. "She got Jessica it, then flew to L.A. and hit on Nick Lachey. When he turned her down, she sued her doctor, claiming that if it'd looked exactly like Jessica's, he would have asked her out."

"My dad represented her and she *won*." Alicia sparkled with pride. "That girl got ten million dollars."

"Per boob?" Dylan asked.

"P.B."

"Yeah, but the key is way more important than twenty million dollars," Massie insisted.

Everyone sighed.

In search of a winning strategy, Massie shut her eyes and practiced yogic breathing—deep inhales and slow, complete exhales. The others waited patiently for her sage words.

After ten high-quality breaths she lifted her head and spoke.

"Blazers. We should definitely wear blazers."

"Definitely," they agreed.

"She's late!" Massie barked at the heavy oak doors of Mr. Rivera's grand, dimly lit study.

"Relax, it's a common negotiating strategy." Alicia, who was nestled in her father's high-back Italian cowhide desk chair, stuck another Ticonderoga No. 2 in the automatic sharpener. "She's trying to heighten your feelings of desperation."

"Huh?" Dylan burped.

"Makes sense." Kristen slid the tall wooden ladder along the towering bookshelves.

"How do *you* know?" Massie hated when the girls acted like they knew things she didn't, especially when they did.

"Psychology for Dummies." She ran a finger along a row of dusty encyclopedias and unfun legal journals. "If Layne's late, you'll worry she's changed her mind. And that will make you panic. Then when she *does* show up, you'll be so relieved you'll give in to her list of demands." She snapped. "Like that."

"Point!" Crossing the leather-scented room, Alicia gathered her tweezer-sharp pencils and set them on the cherry-wood conference table. Fresh yellow legal pads, an emerald green banker's lamp, and a bottle of chilled Evian had been placed in front of every cushy seat. Assorted fruit and cheese platters doubled as centerpieces, while an intercom shaped like a miniature black spacecraft waited patiently at the head of the table in case someone needed to be conferenced in. The only thing missing was the key.

Boop.

A red light appeared on the side of the spacecraft. "Alicia, your one-thirty is here," said the Riveras' housekeeper.

"Thanks, Joyce. Send her—"

"Have her wait," Massie interrupted. She checked her reflection in the silver wine goblets by the minibar. Her hair, pulled into a tight chignon, gave an air of seriousness, which her cropped navy blazer and matching mini echoed. Knee-high argyle socks peeked out of the tops of her leather riding boots, adding a necessary dash of color.

All of a sudden, Layne burst through the double French doors looking like a combination of George Washington and Batman. "I didn't come he-ah to wait."

A gray barrister's wig covered her stringy beige hair. The helmet of tight curls framed her face, then ended in a low ponytail that had been fastened with a black cloth bow. A cape-type gown was draped over her shoulders and tied at her collarbone. Round, lensless wire frames were perched on the bridge of her nose, and a silver lockbox was handcuffed to her wrist.

One-liners popped into Massie's mind with IM swiftness, each one making fun of Layne's costume, her fake British accent, and her overall LBR-ishness. But they would have to wait until the key was dangling from the Coach key chain that was waiting—rather impatiently—in Massie's red quilted Chanel clutch.

"Since Cla-h is in contract nego-si-ations of heh own, I will be representing both of us." She helped herself to a seat at the head of the table.

"Very well, milord." Massie gave a sharp nod to Alicia, signaling that it was time to begin.

She stood, smoothing her winter-white RL blazer, which she'd paired with dark-wash skinny Citizens and brown suede Marc Jacobs flats. "I hereby declare this key meeting now in session. Please rise."

Everyone did.

"You may now take your seats."

"State your terms." Massie gripped her pencil.

After taking a minute to adjust her specs, Layne unrolled a long white sheet of parchment.

"Ech, hem." She cleared her already clear throat. "Cl-ah Lyons and Layne Abeley dema-hnd the following in exchange for this key." She shook the lockbox. The clang made Massie's fingers tingle.

"One. Clah would like to be reinstated into the Pretty Committee.

"Two. Layne would like access to two sleepovers peh month and a guaranteed spoht for hur sleeping bag beside Clah. And she can be in charge of one of thah activities, which might include working with clay, re-creating unfahgettable scenes from Tony Award–winning Broadway shows, or mask making."

Dylan pushed back a sleeve of her dark green velvet blazer and reached for a pineapple slice, dribbling juice from the platter to her chin.

Layne twirled her heart-shaped locket, waiting for Dylan to finish chewing.

"Three. We would like unlimited access to thah 'room.'" She used her pinky fingers to make air quotes as her hands were working to keep the parchment open. "With peh-mission to store poster board, wood, and oth-ah protest-sign materials in said 'room.'

"Foh. In public, you have to pretend you like Heather, Meena, and me."

Answer me, Layne. . . . Answer me, Layne . . . squawked her personalized parrot ringtone.

"I have to take this," she said, momentarily forgetting her accent.

Answer me, Layne. . . . Answer me, Layne. . . .

"Hey! What's up?" asked Layne, as she jammed the cell under her wig, in search of her ear. "Why are you whispering? . . . Well, why are you hiding in the bathroom? . . . How can it be boring when they're talking about all the money they're going to pay you to star in a movie with . . . Yeah, it's going good. . . . I just read number four. . . . Okay, hold on." Layne looked at the intercom. "Claire wants to go on speaker."

"Tell her to call my dad's office. It's the same as our

home number with a nine on the end instead of an eight." Alicia instructed.

"Did you hear that?" Layne asked into the phone. "'Kay, bye."

Five seconds later Claire's voice was coming out of the little black spaceship. "How's it going?"

"It's going good." Layne was the only one who answered. "How's it going over there?"

"Boring," Claire mumbled, her mouth obviously pressed against the speaker. "For the last hour everyone's been arguing about foreign DVD sales. And the food is all sugar-free and low fat. It burns my tongue."

"Poor Princess Nobody." Massie rolled her eyes. "Now can we puh-lease get on with it?" She tapped her pencil.

"Roi-t, roi-t." Layne snapped back into barrister mode and picked up her parchment.

Kristen giggled.

Joyce knocked lightly on the French doors. "Alicia, your sundaes are ready."

"Yay!" Alicia air-clapped.

"You guys are having sundaes?" Claire asked.

"Not everyone has to eat Snackwells." Massie grinned, loving the envy in Claire's voice.

"Ehmagawd!" Dylan stood. "They're make-your-own."

Joyce wheeled in a gold-plated cart filled with an assortment of syrups, sprinkles, ice creams, and crumbled Oreos. A battery-powered blender was on the bottom tier should anyone want to whip her sundae into a blizzard.

"Are those Reese's peanut-butter cups?" Dylan's hands met in prayer position.

"Yes." Joyce lowered her head as if to say, "You're welcome." Her buttery blond bun was the same color as the cupcakes on the cookie platter. She gave each girl a bone china bowl and a long-stemmed silver spoon. "Will that be all?"

"Yup, thanks, J." Alicia smiled warmly at the woman who'd helped raise her since she was three days old.

"Very well." Joyce looked pleased, revealing deep-set crow's-feet in the corners of her kind blue eyes. "Enjoy."

Layne removed her pink retainer, placed it on her legal pad, and pushed back her crimson upholstered wing chair.

"Not so fast." Massie snapped her fingers. Dylan, Kristen, and Alicia hurried to block the cart.

"Why?" Layne eyed the mountain of melting ice cream behind them.

"Not until you're done with the dem-ahhhh-nds."

"I'm done."

"Completely done?"

"Done." Layne licked her lips.

Massie nodded her head once and the girls stepped away.

"Wait!" Claire's voice reverberated from the spaceship. "What about five through ten?"

"We're good." Layne dropped a handful of M&M's in her mouth. The lockbox swung into a platter of peeled bananas, sending them crashing to the ground. "Looks like *those* bananas split." She burst out laughing. Everyone else glared.

"What kind of sundaes are you having?" Claire asked,

ignoring the person in the background knocking on her bathroom door.

"Sweetie, you okay in there?"

"Yeah. Be right out, Mom!"

Everyone snickered.

"Hurry, Ira is about to explain the how the actors' union works."

Claire moaned. "Coming."

"Are those chocolate-covered gummy bears?" Massie said louder than she needed to. "Mmmm."

"They make those?"

"Good luck with your meeting, Claire. See ya." Massie switched off the intercom. "How about a recess?" She took a long sip of her Evian.

"Oops, sorry." Layne covered her mouth, the lockbox dangling from her wrist. "I just ate the last one."

"No." Massie slammed her bottle of water on the table. "I'm saying we need a break. From *you*. We have to discuss the terms."

Layne straightened her wire frames and tucked the lockbox under her armpit. "Of course."

She scooped three helpings of colorful sprinkles onto her strawberry ice cream and hurried out the door.

Kristen unbuttoned her denim A&F blazer and flung it over the back of her chair. "Are we seriously going to give in to *all* four of those demands?"

"'Course nawt." Alicia dropped a stack of dusty legal books on the table. "We're gonna counter."

Dylan licked her spoon. "Meaning?"

"Meaning we argue her list and come back with a new one of our own." Massie nibbled her thumbnail for the first time in years.

"What if she doesn't like our list?" Kristen asked. "What if Layne insists on all or nothing? Then what?"

"Then we'll be making masks on Friday nights and protesting on Sundays." Dylan sighed.

"Point."

"Wrong!" Massie snapped. "We can't compromise the Pretty Committee like that. I'd rather lose the room than sacrifice the things that are important to us."

"Really?" squeaked Alicia.

"Really." Massie exhaled the tsunami of stress that had been wreaking havoc on her insides for the last six days. "What good is a shoe if it doesn't have a sole?"

"Huh?" Dylan seemed to ask for all of them.

"Um, I have a question." Alicia raised her hand. "What if the shoe *has* a sole but no one wants to wear it?"

Massie grinned. "I'll find a way to make people want to wear it. That's what alphas do."

Ten minutes later, Alicia stood. "Layne we've heard your terms. Now hear ours."

She sat.

"Can I get Clah back on the phone?"

Massie nodded at the black spaceship.

Completely unaware of the Oreo chunk dangling from the side of her wig, Layne dialed.

After four rings, Claire picked up. "Mom, I'm going to get some water," she announced. "Be right back."

"I'll have some," said a deep-voiced man.

"Me too," another chimed in. "Make mine with ice."

Claire sighed.

"How's it going?" Layne asked. "How much are they going to pay you?"

"Don't know yet. We're still trying to decide if I should go to summer school or night school."

"Ew to both!" Alicia winced.

"I know."

"Won't you be back here in the fall?" Layne asked.

Massie wrote her name in bubble letters on the cardboard back of her legal pad, pretending not to care.

"No, the final act is being shot in Bhutan. Then in January they want me to go to Japan to do press junkets. You know, so I'll have experience when it's time to do them here."

"Sayonara." Massie waved to the spaceship, placing all her hope in reverse psychology. "Now can we puh-lease move on?"

"Ugh! I hate my *hair*," Claire whispered.

"No argument here." Massie flipped through her notes. "We hate your hair too."

Alicia, Dylan, and Kristen snickered.

"I said," Claire whisper-shouted, "I *hate* that I'm not *there*."

"Don't worry, it will grow back eventually." Massie lifted her legal pad. "Here are the terms set forth by the Pretty Committee."

Layne pulled a feathered quill and a tiny jar of red ink out of her wool kneesock and set them on the table.

"One. Claire may be reinstated into the Pretty Committee."

Claire squeaked with joy.

"As *long*," Massie continued, "as she apologizes for lying about Cam's uncle and—"

"I'm sorry." Claire sounded choked up. "I will never ever do anything like—"

"Forgiven," Massie interrupted. "*And* as long as she remains in Westchester. If she moves, she's out."

Layne dipped her quill, then scribbled on her parchment.

"Two. Layne can go to one sleepover per month, not two. And we *will* make fun of her, only if she insists on working with clay, re-creating unforgettable scenes from Tony Award–winning Broadway shows, or making masks."

Claire giggled.

Layne opened her mouth, but Massie cut her off. "And yes, she can put her sleeping bag beside Claire's—so long as Claire is *there*. That's a given."

Layne lowered her head and wrote.

"Three. Unlimited access to the room has been denied. Permission to store poster board and other sign-making materials has been granted, so long as they are kept in a suitcase made by Louis Vuitton or Coach.

"Four. We cannot and will not promise to pretend we like you in public."

Layne slammed down her quill.

"If we like you, we will act like it. If we don't, we won't."

"Fine." Layne resumed writing.

Alicia stood. "That's our offer. Take it or leave it."

She sat.

"I have one more thing," Claire said. "No more eyebrow jokes."

Layne bit down on her locket.

"You mean we can't refer to them as the Bush twins anymore?" Massie snickered.

"No!"

"Hmmmm." Massie rubbed her chin like she was mulling it over. "On one condition." She glared at Layne. "Is the picture of Tricky still inside that locket?"

Layne spit it out of her mouth and nodded.

"Wipe it off and give it to me."

The way Alicia, Dylan, and Kristen looked at her, Massie might as well have borrowed Claire's Keds.

"Why do you want *this*?" Layne clutched the gold necklace.

Massie wiggled her fingers. "Deal or no deal?"

"Will you stop making fun of my clothes?" Layne asked.

"I'll try."

"No deal." Layne popped it back in her mouth.

"Okay, fine. Deal."

"And you'll compliment me in public?" she pressed, slowly removing the heart-shaped locket from between her wet lips.

"Fine, fine, whatevs." Massie held out her hand and wiggled her fingers. "Just give it to me before your saliva burns a hole though it."

Carefully, Layne lifted the tarnished gold chain over her wig and slid it across the table.

Ignoring her friends' puzzled glares, Massie picked it up with a piece of legal paper, disenfected it with Evian, and then dropped it in her clutch. "Looks like we're all done here."

"One more thing." Alicia walked a stapled document over to Layne. "This confidentiality agreement was created by my father, Len Rivera, a *lawyer*." Alicia folded her arms across her chest. "You and Claire need to sign it."

"What is it?"

"It says you will never, ever, ever tell another human being, dead or alive, that you found the key before we did. This fact—which we are about to erase from the history books—should never appear in print, code, tattoos, foreign languages, or journals, or on handheld or desk-based electronic devices, billboards, or T-shirts, or engraved on jewelry or anything else we haven't thought of."

Layne dipped her quill and scrawled her name at the bottom of the document.

"Kuh-laire." Alicia blew Layne's signature dry. "Massie will bring this over for you to sign later this afternoon."

"'Kay."

"Great. Then are we done?" Layne unclipped her cape.

"Not quite."

"Oh." Layne untied the black bow that held the low ponytail in her wig and dangled it above Massie's palm. A tiny key hung off the end. "Will you unlock me?" She held out her wrist, which was still handcuffed to the metal safe.

"Given." Massie unlocked Layne's handcuffs and then grabbed the box that held the key to her future.

THE BLOCK ESTATE
THE GUESTHOUSE
Saturday, April 10th
4:26 P.M.

"Signature, please." Massie thrust a piece of paper and a black Montblanc fountain pen in Claire's face the instant she opened the guesthouse door.

"Hey!" She folded her arms across her mint green J. Crew oxford. In her denim Gap miniskirt and pineapple-covered Keds, Claire looked like a sweet suburban schoolgirl. It was her attempt to remind the lawyers she wasn't a gorilla, even though she resembled one from the neck up.

"Where were you?" Massie pushed past her and entered the Lyonses' house like she owned it, which technically she did. "I've been calling. I thought you were supposed to be home all day planning your big Hollywood *career*." She said *career* like most people would say *snot*.

Embarrassed by the mess of coffee mugs and stacks of crumb-filled plates the lawyers had left behind on the dining room table, Claire guided Massie toward the stairs.

"They left an hour ago, so my mom took me to CVS. We just got back." Claire swung the crinkly drugstore bag like a limited-edition Chanel.

"Whatevs." Massie shrugged. "As soon as you sign this confidentiality agreement, I'll be out of your *hair*."

"Hey! No eyebrow jokes. You promised."

"Ooops, sorry." She quickly covered her mouth. "I forgot."

"Well, then, I'm not signing." Throwing the CVS bag over her shoulder, Claire turned and stomped up the creaky wood stairs. An afternoon with cutthroat Hollywood lawyers had inspired her to hold her ground and stick up for herself.

"Okay, wait." Massie raced toward the staircase.

Claire stopped.

"It's just that—" Massie fake-sobbed. "It's just that I'm gonna miss those jokes." She giggled.

"We're done." Claire hurried into the bathroom, slamming the door behind her.

The soles of Massie's riding boots beating against the wooden stairs as she climbed to the top, sounded like a fierce game of Ping-Pong.

"I'm sorry, okay?" she called. "Open up."

Claire paused and examined herself in the mirrored medicine cabinet. Coarse black hair and two wiry black strips above her eyes stared back. A mosaic of honey yellow tiles filled the background. The towels that hung on the silver rod behind her were also yellow, as was the shag bath mat and the matching toilet-seat cover. She felt like a fuzzy bumblebee in a Pine-Sol–scented hive.

"Kuh-laire, come awn!" Massie shook the silver door handle.

"Only if you promise not to make fun of me anymore."

"Done."

"I don't believe you."

"Pinky-swear."

Claire turned the lock and opened the door, just enough to sick out her pinky. Massie reached for it and shook.

"Now sign." Massie slapped the confidentiality agreement on the white marble countertop. Placing the pen on top of it, she pointed the gold nib to the exact spot Claire needed to sign.

"I'll need a minute to vet this." Claire used her lawyer's word for *examine* like it was a term they tossed around on IM twenty times a day.

"Given."

Massie sat on the toilet-seat cover. She unbuttoned her burgundy blazer and pulled a platinum chain out of her barely there cleavage, giving way to a clumpy awkward necklace. A cluster of pastel-colored enamel handbags hung alongside a red leather tag, stamped with the boxy Coach logo. It was exactly what Skye had asked for in her video, right down to the dangling gold key. "Next year is going to be so ah-mazing. This room is gonna mean automatic A-list in high school."

Claire ignored her attempts to provoke jealousy, pretending to vet the agreement.

"Remember that tunnel you were talking about?"

Claire kept moving her eyes across the words (twelve-point Courier, bold, and all caps), with grave intensity, the way her lawyer had done with her studio contract. "Well, we're already working on plans to build it, you know, so Cam can sneak in during lunch."

"Mmmm." Claire flipped the page.

"It's too bad you won't be here." Massie stood. "We have tons of plans. We were gonna get a gummy bear dispenser. But now that you're leaving, there's kinda no point."

Claire tried to steady the corners of her mouth. It was obvious Massie was upset she was leaving. And it was making her smile.

"Looks good to me." She scribbled her name under Layne's and snapped the black cap back on the weighty pen. "Congratulations. It sounds like the room is gonna be cool." She reached into the plastic bag and pulled out a box of Revlon's Frost & Glow blonding kit.

"Cool?" Massie looked her in the eye for the first time since the eyebrow extensions.

"Yeah." Claire tore open the package and snapped on the protective gloves. "It sounds like you'll have a fun year."

"Doesn't that bum you out at *all*?"

"No." She mixed the blonding powder with the blonding cream. "Why should it?"

"'Cause you're not going to be part of it."

Claire tied a yellow towel around her shoulders like a cape. "Send pictures." She painted a thick band of white paste over her scalp.

Massie's glossy mouth hung open. "That's it? *Send pictures?* That's all you have to say?" She shut her eyes for a split second and gently shook her head no in a this-can't-be-happening sort of way. "What about Cam?"

"What *about* him?" Twisting and contorting, Claire

struggled to reach the back of her head. A glob of dye landed between her collarbones, missing her hair entirely.

"Doesn't he want you to stay?" Massie grabbed the dye brush from Claire's hands and dipped it in the mix.

"Yeah." Claire turned, surrendering to Massie. "But he's the only one." She pulled off the gloves and handed them over.

"You mean if other people wanted you to stay, you would?" Massie gathered a handful of black hair and covered it with dye. Then, she massaged it into the hair, making sure the color was evenly distributed.

"I dunno." Claire bit her lower lip. "Maybe."

"I bet your family'll miss you."

"Why? They'd go with me."

"Oh." Massie massaged harder. "Well, what about Layne?"

"She'll visit." Claire pulled a pair of little silver scissors from her bag and ripped off the cardboard wrapper.

"What about Kristen and Alicia and Dylan? I heard them say they want you to stay." Massie snapped a shower cap on Claire's head.

"Yeah, right." Claire leaned in toward the mirror. "When you kicked me out of the Pretty Committee, they didn't care one bit." Raising the silver scissors, she snipped the thin black thread that had been woven into her brows. A flurry of coarse black hair fell past her blond lashes. Then—*snip, snip, snip*—more hair dusted the rim of the white porcelain sink.

Fussing with the tangle of handbag charms around her neck, Massie murmured, "Well, I'd prob'ly miss you."

"What'd you say?" Claire asked, desperate to hear Massie's confession a second time, to make sure it was real.

"I said"—she rolled her eyes—"I'd pro-ba-bly miss you."

Even though Claire's paste-covered hair was stuffed in a shower cap and her left eyebrow was blond while the other was black and bushy, she felt more confident than she had in her entire life.

"That's what I thought you said."

"So does this mean you'll stay?"

There was a loud pounding on the door.

"Open up. It's an emergency!"

"Use the one downstairs, Todd!"

The girls covered their mouths and giggled.

"No!" He jiggled the handle. "I need to talk to you. It's about the lawyers."

"What?"

"Open!"

Claire rolled her eyes and cracked open the door. "Speak."

Todd burst in.

"What are you wearing?" Massie pinched the lapel of his white linen sport coat and rubbed it between her fingers. "You know it's only April, right?"

"So?" Todd smoothed a hand over the side part in his orange hair.

"*So?* That's a summer suit." Massie snickered. "And what's with the three-quarter sleeves?"

"It's vintage."

"What do you want?" Claire barked, resenting her younger brother for interrupting their most heartfelt moment ever.

"I *want* to talk to the lawyers."

"'Bout what?"

"Emancipating me from Mom and Dad."

"Why?" the girls asked at the exact same time.

"Because I've been grounded for thirty-three days and it's totally unfair."

"No, it's not." Claire pushed her brother toward the open door. "You skipped school, hid in the back of the Range Rover, and stowed away on our trip to *The Daily Grind*. It's *totally* fair."

"I have a case. I want to divorce Mom and Dad and live on my own."

"Well, you'll have to find another lawyer."

"And another suit," Massie added.

"Why?" Todd stomped his forest green Converse high-tops.

"Because I told the lawyers to leave." Claire looked at Massie. "For good."

"Huh?" Massie asked Claire's blond eyebrows, as if noticing them for the first time.

"I quit the movie."

"What?" Todd and Massie yelled in unison.

"I told them I wanted to stay." Claire's heart pounded, just like it had in Lake Placid right before she kissed Cam for the first time. "In Westchester. At OCD. With you guys.

And Cam. I'm tired of missing out on everything. And I'm over looking like a Brillo pad."

"Yes!" Massie air-clapped and bounced on her toes.

"You turned down a major motion picture?" Todd slapped his hand against his forehead. "Are you crazy?"

"Maybe." Claire smiled peacefully.

"I definitely want out of this family!" Todd stormed into the hallway, slamming the door behind him.

Massie checked her silver Coach Whitney watch and then, without a word, removed the cap from Claire's head. "Why didn't you tell me you were going to stay?"

"Why didn't you tell me you were going to miss me?"

"Point." Massie lifted her finger in the air, Alicia style.

Claire giggled and pulled Massie in for a hug.

The instant Massie hugged back, Claire knew she'd made the right decision. The Pretty Committee was going to dominate the eighth grade. And what could possibly be more fun than that?

Cam leaned forward in his seat, raised his A&W root beer, and rested a warm hand on his girlfriend's shoulder. "To blond Claire and the end of her movie career."

"For now," she giggle-warned.

Alicia, Dylan, Derrington, and Josh clinked waxy paper cups. "To blond Claire."

While everyone toasted the good news, Massie lowered her black Stella McCartney sunglasses and raised the rim on her olive green army cap.

Skye was one section over, to their right, surrounded by the DSL Daters. All five girls wore identical gray stretch pants, black ballet slippers, and different-colored slouchy knit sweaters. Gold bangles, braided macramé bracelets, leather bands, and platinum link chains lined their arms like mismatched sleeves. Rumor had it they added a new bracelet every time one of them kissed a boy. Judging from the swarm of cute high school guys buzzing around them, a visit to Tiffany was minutes away.

"I'm going to the bathroom." Massie stood.

"Again?" Derrington asked from the row of bleachers behind her. "You've gone like ten times in the last hour.

Besides, I have something to show you." He pulled a tiny silver camera from the pocket of his A&F camo shorts.

"Can it wait?" Massie pushed her glasses back up, shielding her eyes from the blazing sun. Even if she hadn't been repulsed by Derrington's bedroom—which she so had—she would have hit pause on his little show-and-tell. She had more important things to deal with.

Claire, who was sitting in the boys' row sharing a bag of peanuts with Cam, leaned forward and whispered in Massie's ear. "You've been walking by her all afternoon flashing that key. She hasn't said a word."

Massie sighed. Claire was right. Skye was ignoring her. What if she knew Layne found the key first? Or what if she was holding a grudge because Massie had approached her? The cold-shoulder thing was giving her serious chills. It was time to put her secret plan into effect and pray that it didn't backfire.

"Block." Derrington kicked her bleacher. "Check this out." He thrust the camera in her face but Massie waved it away. "I have to go."

She scurried past her friends' denim-clad legs and raced up to the LBR Jr. section, five rows behind her.

"Todd, can I talk to you for a minute?"

The ten-year-old was sandwiched between Tiny Nathan and some kid wearing a floppy red-and-white-striped Cat in the Hat hat.

"It's important."

His friends teased him with a chorus of *woo-hooo*s, *awww yeahhh*s, and kissy sounds.

Massie folded her arms across her chest and tapped her black suede Miu Miu clogs, letting him know this was serious business.

"I need a favor." She dragged him to the very top row.

Todd puckered his lips.

"Ew, nawt that." She smacked his light blue Orlando Magic cap. "This."

Massie handed him an ah-dorable pink vellum envelope. Inside was Layne's gold locket, complete with the picture of Tricky and a note that said:

SKYE,
    HERE is the pony you asked for. ONE
day I hope I can get you the REAL thing.
            HAPPY graduation,
                xo CHRis Abeley
PS—PlEASE don't thANK mE. EvER! I REAlly
mEAN it! PlEASE don't! I'm vERy vERy shy.

"Go give this to Skye and I guarantee she'll give you another kiss. Only this time it will be in front of everyone."

"Really?" Todd's face lit up.

"Yup." Massie grabbed his scrawny shoulders and glared into his dark eyes. "But you can't tell her it came from me. If she asks where you got it, tell her some high school guy paid you to deliver it."

"And she'll kiss me?"

Massie nodded. "Vigorously."

"In front of everyone?"

"Yup, now go!" She practically kicked him down the bleachers.

"Watch this!" he shouted to his friends when he passed.

Casually, Massie returned to her seat.

"What's *he* doing there?" Claire gasped, noticing her brother tapping Skye's shoulder, trying to distract her from a shaggy blond clutching a gray skateboard.

"That kid is my hero," Josh snickered.

Alicia rolled her eyes.

The Pretty Committee stood, mouths agape, as Skye broke away from the skater, took the envelope from Todd, and read the note. Seconds later, she handed the package to the DSL Daters, who fanned their faces and squealed like they were holding an invitation to Zac Efron's birthday party. As promised, Skye threw her decorated arms around the redhead and gave him a juicy kiss on the lips. Todd turned to his friends and threw his fists in the air.

They cheered like he'd just scored the winning goal.

"What was that all about?" Alicia asked in shock.

"I dunno, but it looks like someone's getting a new bracelet," Massie whisper-smiled to herself.

Once seated, she pulled the Coach key-chain necklace out of her burnt orange Barneys cashmere sweater vest, lifted it over her head, and twirled. The tiny handbags smashed into her knuckles and the chain coiled around her index finger, practically cutting off all circulation to her hand.

"Yes!" Josh jumped to his feet along with the rest of the navy-and-yellow-clad Sirens fans.

"Goal!" Derrington wiggled his butt while Cam and Josh smacked it.

Only the Pretty Committee remained seated.

"Get up," insisted Derrington. "Kristen just scored."

"She did?" Massie she climbed up on the bleacher with the rest of the Sirens fans. A soccer-ball-size lump of pride stuck in her throat as she cheered for her ex-teammates and one of her best friends. "Numba seven!"

"One-nothing for the Sirens!" Claire shouted.

"People who don't know us must think we're real fans." Dylan clapped.

"Puh-lease." Massie rolled her eyes. "Everyone knows us."

"Point!" Alicia giggled.

The crowd settled. And the game was back on.

"We totally used to be on that team," Alicia told two eighth-grade girls in front of her.

They gave her a heartfelt thumbs-up.

"Foot long!" called a girl dressed in a pink Splendid hoodie. She had wavy brown hair, full, high-glossed lips, and cool gold aviators—hardly the stadium-vendor type. "Pass it to Ms. Stella McCartney Glasses over there." She placed the foil-wrapped dog in Dylan's hands.

Massie felt her cheeks redden. "Ew, I so didn't order *that*," she announced to the people around her.

"Yes, you did," insisted the vendor.

"I did nawt! I don't *do* street meat."

"Eat it!" she insisted before flipping on her hood and sprinting down the steps.

"Who *was* that?" Alicia asked out the side of her mouth.

"Probably some LBR who wants me to get fat."

"Point."

"I'll eat it." Claire waved her hand in the space between Dylan and Alicia's heads.

"Sharing is caring. Let's split it," insisted Dylan as she peeled back the foil. "Eh. Ma. Gawd." She held the hot dog across Alicia's lap, lifting it toward Massie's face. "Look!"

"Yes!"

Assuming the Sirens had scored another goal, some LBRs in their section jumped to their feet.

"False alarm." Dylan motioned for them to sit.

"Lemme see." Claire's poked her head between Massie and Alicia.

Written with spicy brown mustard, in what they assumed to be Skye's beautiful loopy script, it said, 4 p.m. storage shed.

Excitement in the stands started to build. Sirens fans were sliding to the edges of the bleachers, hollering and clapping. It was as if everyone had gotten mustard messages from Skye.

Kristen was charging down the field dribbling the ball. She circled around a stocky Meerkat, did a kick-fall, and shot the ball straight into the white net.

"That's the game!" Derrington smacked Massie's shoulder. Everyone cheered and hugged and chanted Kristen's name.

"She's our best friend!" Dylan shouted.

"We used to be on the team," Alicia announced again.

"We're going to the finals!" Claire yelled as she and Cam punched the mild spring air.

Casually, as if removing a mascara booger from the corner of her eye, Massie reached under her sunglasses and wiped away a happy relief drop. Now Kristen was famous too.

"Block." Derrington stepped onto her bleacher, then hopped down beside her. "Will you *please* look at this?" He turned on his digital camera and shielded the tiny screen from the glaring sun.

"Fine." Massie lifted her oval glasses. She was looking at a boring shot of a navy-comforter-covered bed and a hay-colored sisal rug. "So what? It's a room. I'm not even in it."

"It's *my* room." He beamed. "I cleaned it for you."

Suddenly Massie's stomach dipped, like she was riding one of the sea-tossed sailboats etched in his tin headboard.

He cared.

"Wanna come over after the game and see it in person?" His brown eyes were wide with hope, like a little boy asking his mom for a chocolate-chip cookie before dinner.

"I would, but there's something I have to do."

"Cool." He turned, in search of his friends. "I better go and—"

"How about tomorrow? After school."

Derrington wiggled his butt.

"Let me go." Kristen struggled to break free from Dylan's grip. "I have to shower."

"We don't have time!" Massie helped drag her through the crowd.

"But some people wanted my autograph." Kristen looked back at the cluster of fans on the field, surrounding her teammates. "And the coach is taking us out for—"

"We're meeting Skye," Massie whispered in her sweaty ear.

"Ehmagawd! Skye contacted—?"

Massie slapped her hand in front of Kristen's mouth. They had come too far to blow it now.

The sound of excited chatter faded into the distance as they rapidly crossed campus, finally giving the girls a minute to talk freely.

"I can't believe she wrote the message on a hot dog," Kristen gasped while wiping her forehead with a pink-and-orange Puma sweatband.

"I can't believe Coach Davis made you captain for next year," Claire panted.

"I know." Kristen folded the elastic on her navy shorts, revealing her flat, pale abs. "I'm—"

187

"Less talking, more walking." Massie grabbed Kristen's clammy hand, then checked over her shoulder. "Hurry, Leesh. We can't be late."

"I'm try-ing, o-kay?" She pumped her arms.

"I see them!" Dylan stopped to shake a pebble from her ruby red ballet flats, then pointed at the wood storage shed between the tennis courts and the school's basement entrance.

"Where?" Alicia broke into a light trot.

"On the roof." Dylan gazed at the five girls sunning themselves in a perfect line, each with one leg bent.

Massie immediately slowed her pace to a casual mall-wander.

"How'd they get up there?" Kristen squinted.

"How'd they get heather gray leggings?" Dylan asked. "They're the hardest color to find."

Alicia huffed. "I bet Skye got them from Body Alive."

"Whatevs." Massie smoothed a coat of Glossip Girl Original Bubble Gum across her lips, then pinched her cheeks for a burst of natural color. She would become a confident alpha in three . . . two . . . one—

"We're here!"

Skye lifted her head and snapped three times.

One by one, the all-blond quintet leaped off the roof, each one landing gracefully on the blue gymnastics tumbling mat that had been strategically placed below the shed. One had braids, two had long ponytails, and another had a voluminous bob. Skye was the DSL Dater with long thick waves, and the only one Massie envied.

She sauntered over to greet them, toes pointed in second position and clutching the gold locket.

The other blondes followed.

Massie grinned, projecting confidence. Without a word, she pulled the Coach key chain out of her oversize orange V-necked sweater and let it slam against her chest.

"Nice work," Skye grinned.

"Nice work," echoed the DSL Daters.

Relief hugged Massie like a pair of skintight Sass & Bide jeans.

"Ready to go?" Skye pushed up one sleeve of her angora pink sweater. Among the tangle of bracelets, a black satin blindfold lay wrapped around her wrist. She pulled it off, letting it dangle from her index finger. The DSL Daters did the same.

"Ready," the Pretty Committee answered.

All of a sudden, Massie's eyes were being covered to the clang of Skye's gold bangles. "Hey, what are you doing?" Kristen squealed.

"Shhh," hissed one of the DSL Daters. "By the way, good game today. You were awesome."

"Thanks," she giggle-gushed.

"Ow. Stop pulling me," Alicia whined.

"Leesh, is that you?" Dylan asked.

"No." Claire laughed. "It's me. Get your hand off my butt."

"Ooops, sorry."

"No talking!" Skye snapped. "If we get caught, it's over.

Now let's move." She gripped Massie's elbow and led her across the grass.

"Easy," Massie pleaded. "I'm in clogs."

Skye slowed her pace.

Panic was starting to set in, and breathing suddenly became painful; each shallow inhalation bit Massie's lungs like an overexcited puppy. What if people were watching them and laughing? What if the Pretty Committee was being set up and the whole key thing was a joke? What if she tripped? Desperate for saliva, Massie licked her bubble-gum-flavored lips. But nothing came. Even her spit was starting to panic.

"Do we really need these blindfolds?"

Skye smacked Massie's wandering hand, delivering a fresh waft of Clinique's Happy perfume straight to her nostrils. "You can't see where the room is until I know you have the real key."

"Puh-lease!" Massie turned to Skye, even though her eyes were covered. "I don't *do* fake!"

"None of us do!" Alicia insisted.

Skye tightened her grip, silently forbidding Massie to say another word.

The familiar pump of the horizontal handle—found only on the door to the gym, the side entrance, and the pool—assured Massie that they were still on OCD grounds.

"Ow! Watch the toes," Dylan snapped.

"Shhhhh," hissed one of the DSL Daters.

Suddenly, everything felt dark. The air around them was

no longer fresh. It smelled like a mix of orange-scented floor wax and the inside of a tuna lover's lunch box.

"Are we by the loser lockers?" Alicia asked.

Dylan sniffed. "More like the janitor's room."

"Mass, what do you think?" Kristen asked.

"E-nough," Skye hissed.

Massie didn't care where they were. As long as they were getting closer—closer to their secret campus club-house, closer to their fabulous future, closer to eighth-grade domination.

After one hundred and thirty-nine paces across a slick floor, a walk down a short ramp, and two flights of stairs, they reached their destination—a damp room that reeked of wet cardboard.

"We're here." Skye shimmied Massie between the smell of Angel perfume (Alicia?) and Finesse shampoo (Claire?).

"Ready?"

"Yes," the Pretty Committee said together.

Massie was overcome by pre-present tingles, a flutter she'd get in her stomach just before tearing the wrapping paper off her birthday presents. To her, nothing was better than that sliver of time that hung between expectation and reality. Because in that sliver, anything was possible.

"Okay," Skye trumpeted. "Blindfolds off!"

It took a moment for Massie's mascara-covered lashes to unstick and her eyes to focus. When they finally did, the DSL Daters were huddled around the girls, keeping them from seeing anything in the dim corridor.

Skye held out her hand. "Key."

Massie slapped the necklace in her smooth white palm and grinned.

Alicia squeaked.

Dylan twirled a curl.

Kristen twisted her sweatband.

And Claire bit her thumbnail.

After a back bend, a neck roll and some quick calf stretches, Skye stepped up to the silver handle. The DSL Daters parted just enough for the Pretty Committee to see the blue door in front of them.

"Before I open the room, I need you to understand that you are about to become members of an exclusive club."

Massie curled her toes to keep from leaping.

"If you get caught in here, you will have ruined a sacred, time-honored tradition, and all the past key holders will unite and make your lives miserable."

"Don't worry, we *never* get caught." Massie hooked her hair behind one ear.

"Aren't you the girls that got expelled?" asked Braids.

The others giggled.

"We got back in, didn't we?" Massie countered.

"I guess," murmured Braids.

"Don't worry." Alicia looked straight into Skye's intensely turquoise eyes. "The room will be safe with us."

"Good." Skye stuck the key in the lock. She jiggled it to the right. Then the left.

A prickly sweat rushed Massie's armpits.

"It's not opening." Skye tugged the handle.

Massie immediately cut Claire with her eyes, silently threatening to destroy her life—and her afterlife—if she and Layne had given her the wrong key. "Let me try." She stepped forward.

Skye burst out laughing. "Just kidding!"

The DSL Daters high-fived.

Massie tried her best to giggle.

Skye poked the key in the hole again: This time, it entered without a problem. Then, with a single click, the door unlocked. "Welcome to private-school paradise."

Massie reached her hand inside the dark room and flicked on the lights. Alicia, Claire, Dylan, and Kristen stepped forward.

Everyone gasped.

"Did I lie?" Skye gushed.

Massie tried to answer but couldn't find the words.

No one could.

Q & A

When will THE CLIQUE be a movie? Can I please play Massie?

Everyone asks this question. EVERYONE! And I wish I had better news for you. I really do. All I know is that there are powerful, suit-wearing people in Hollywood trying to make this happen. But until they do, you'll have to keep reading the books and imagine yourself saying the lines. As soon as I get an update I will post it on LisiHarrison. net. Pinky-swear.

And for all you wannabe Massies out there: Practice your comebacks and keep honing your inner queen bee. That way you'll be ready if opportunity knocks!

Who are the girls on the cover supposed to be?

Is the one in the middle Massie or Alicia? Where is Claire? And why are there only three of them and not four? The girls on the covers are models, meant to represent a clique, not *the* Clique. It's up to you to decide based on my description and your imagination what Massie, Claire, Alicia, Kristen, and Dylan look like. So if the girl in the middle looks like Alicia to you, then fine, she's Alicia. And if she doesn't then that's fine too. Whatevs.

Which character is most like you?

I kind of have all the characters in me to some extent. I'm like Massie because I love fashion, clever comebacks, and my puppy Bee Bee. But I am not a bully and would never want to make anyone cry, especially my friends.

I'm like Claire because I try to accept myself for who I am.

I'm like Dylan because I think burps are funny and I love to eat.

I'm like Layne because I think unique is chic. And I go through food obsession phases. This week I can't get enough of those little egg rolls filled with pizza.

The characters I am not like at all are Kristen because I stink at sports and Alicia because I have small boobs and I would never follow anyone.

How are you able to write for seventh graders when you are clearly no longer in the seventh grade?

Simple. I *WAS* in the seventh grade at one point in my life and I remember what it feels like to wake up in the morning and wonder if my friends will still like me, even though I did nothing wrong. I also remember what it feels like to gang up on someone else because, well, better them than me, right? We've all been Massies and we've all been Claires at one point or another, and those feelings of abusing and being abused never go away.

How did you come up with the idea to write about cliques?

I worked at MTV for ten years, and it reminded me a lot of middle school. People were always trying to fit in with the "cool" crowd, and it brought back a lot of memories. I'd hear things like, *Who are you hanging out with this weekend? Did you get invited to any cool parties? Where did you buy that outfit? Who did you eat lunch with today?*

Sound familiar? It wasn't long before I realized that cliques and the desire to be accepted don't go away when you get older. They just get easier to laugh at. And that's why I wrote *THE CLIQUE* as a comedy and not a heart-wrenching drama. Sometimes the way we act is so pathetic it's funny.

Any advice for wannabe writers?

1. Write every day. It doesn't have to be good or interesting or grammatically correct. Just write anyway. It will keep your juices flowing, and I guarantee that by the end of each session you will have at least one good sentence that you can use in the future.

2. Read a lot. And read the stuff you like, not the stuff you *think* you should like. Because chances are you will write in the genre you like to read. So it's important to know how other people are doing it.

3. Carry a little notebook everywhere you go. If you see something funny, write it down. If you meet someone with a cool name, write it down. If you think of an interesting story idea while you're on the bus, write it down. Get it? So the next time you're racking your brain for details or ideas they will be right there in your ah-dorable little notebook.

4. If someone tells you you'll never be a writer, put on your pointiest boots, take a deep breath, and kick them in the shin.

Write about *that*!

How many CLIQUE books will there be?

Right now there will be eight. But if you want more, I'll write more.

Are you going to write other stuff?

Totally! I am always thinking of new and different ideas. My next novel is about fifteen-year-olds at summer camp.

Any advice for people that go to clique-y schools?

For starters, you have to understand why mean girls are mean.

They are insecure.

I know that's hard to believe because they're probably pretty, popular, stylish, and outgoing. But trust me, it's true. Girls who put other girls down do it to feel better about themselves. So keep that in mind next time a pack of wild meanie weenies treats you like a loser. Know that they are the pathetic ones and simply walk away. And stop, stop, stop trying to be accepted by them. Do you seriously think you'd be happier if you were friends with them? Puh-lease!

Go find someone who shares your real interests and hang with her or him. It's better to have one real friend than a hundred fake ones. Given!

Where can I get the Glossip Girl lip gloss you write about in **Invasion of the Boy Snatchers***?*

Sorry, sisters. I made the whole thing up. I only wish there were a Lip-Gloss-of-the-Day Club that delivered a new flavor of gloss to my front door every morning. But until then, just imagine you're getting it. And while you're at it, can you think of some cool new flavors? I'm running out of ideas.

Done. Done. And Done.

Essay

My Life Story

By Lisi Harrison

Any time someone starts a story with, "I was born in...," my eyes glaze over and I try not to yawn in their face. So I'll do my best to find a more interesting way of letting you know I was born and raised in Toronto, Canada.

There, how was that? :)

I did not go to a private school like OCD and I was not in a rich evil clique of "Massies". I went to Hebrew school until ninth grade and then switched to Forest Hill Collegiate, a public high school. A lot of the kids in my grade came from families with tons of money and wore Polo everything (it was really IN back then, okay?). I, on the other hand, was forbidden to wear anything made by anyone other than Kmart or Hanes. I probably would have been allowed to wear The GAP but it wasn't on every block in Canada yet. My parents were on a mission to keep me as grounded and un-spoiled as they possibly could. And now, as much as I ah-dore fashion, I never buy designer clothes or bags. I tend to go for the more original styles. Granted, sometimes I look like a total goof bag but at least I'm the only goof bag at the party.

When I was eighteen I moved to Montreal to become a film major at McGill University. Canadians like to think of it as the Harvard of Canada, but Americans always laugh and call me an "intellectual wannabe" when I say that. Nice, eh?

Anyway, I left McGill after two years because I knew deep

down inside I wanted to be a writer, not a filmmaker, and McGill had a lame creative writing program. So I transferred to Emerson College in Boston, where I graduated with a Bachelor of Fine Arts in creative writing. YAY!

So there I was with a BFA, ten dollars in my LeSportsac, and no plan. Luckily, my friend Lawrence (I call him Larry even though he hates it) was working at MTV in New York and felt sorry for me. He offered me a casting job on a game show called Lip Service. All I had to do was move to Manhattan—the next day.

Um, okay.

I ended up staying at MTV for twelve great years. I had every brutal job there was and eventually worked my way up to head writer and then senior director of development. That's when things got really cool. It was my job to create and develop new shows for the network, including *One Bad Trip* and *Room Raiders*. And believe it or not, it was MTV, not middle school that inspired me to write THE CLIQUE. There were so many employees at MTV who would do and wear anything just to be accepted by the so-called "cool people." It reminded me so much of life in the seventh grade I had to write about it. And the rest is history.

I wrote *The Clique* and *Best Friends for Never* while I was still at MTV, just in case my life as an author didn't work out. And in June 2004 I decided to take the plunge, quit my job, and write full-time.

Now I spend about nine hours a day writing in my New York City apartment, where I am currently working away on book number eight in the series (August '07). I am also trying to get my long-haired Chihuahua Bee Bee to stop licking my computer screen. I should probably take her out for a pee.

Bye!

"I ah-dored *Bass Ackwards and Belly Up*. It's about four BFFs who, for a juicy reason I won't divulge, decide to not go to college to pursue their dreams. It's one of those things most of us fantasize about but don't have the guts to do."

—**Lisi Harrison,** author of the #1 *New York Times* bestselling **CLIQUE** series

Harper Waddle, Sophie Bushell, and Kate Foster are about to commit the ultimate suburban sin—bailing on college to pursue their dreams. Middlebury-bound Becca Winsberg is convinced her friends have gone insane…until they remind her she just might have a dream of her own. So what if their lives are bass ackwards and belly up? They'll always have each other.

BASS ACKWARDS AND BELLY UP ✦ AVAILABLE NOW

More great reads
for fans of THE CLIQUE

BASS ACKWARDS AND BELLY UP
a novel by Elizabeth Craft and Sarah Fain

Harper Waddle, Sophie Bushell, and Kate Foster are about to commit the ultimate suburban sin—bailing on college to pursue their dreams. Middlebury-bound Becca Winsberg is convinced her friends have gone insane . . . until they remind her she just might have a dream of her own. So what if their lives are bass ackwards and belly up? They'll always have each other.

a novel by Alisa Valdes-Rodriguez

From the first day at her new Southern California high school, Pasquala Rumalda de Archuleta ("Paski") learns that the popular students may be diverse in ethnicity but are alike in their cruelty. While Paski tries to concentrate on mountain biking and not thinking too much about ultra-hot Chris Cabrera, she is troubled by the beautiful and wicked Jessica Nguyen. Here at Aliso Niguel High, money is everything and the Haters rule.

secrets OF MY HOLLYWOOD LIFe

a novel by Jen Calonita

What if . . . Your picture were taped inside teenage boys' lockers across America, your closets were bursting with never-worn designer clothing, and the tabloids constantly asked whether you were losing your "good girl" status?

It's a glamorous life, but sixteen-year-old Kaitlin Burke, costar of one of the hottest shows on TV, is exhausted from the pressures of fame. Then she hits on an outrageously daring solution, one that has to remain top secret or it will jeopardize everything she's ever worked for.

Nothing But the Truth
(and a few white lies)

a novel by Justina Chen Headley

Hapa (half Asian and half white) Patty Ho has nothing but problems. She has a super-strict mom, and thanks to a belly button-reading fortune-teller, she's been shipped off to math camp for the summer. But Patty will be challenged by more than arithmetic as she makes new friends, finds a first love, and discovers the truth about her past.

Available wherever books are sold.
www.lb-teens.com

Hachette Book Group USA

Read all the novels in the #1 *New York Times* bestselling series

THE CLIQUE

THE CLIQUE

Massie Block is happily ruling her fabulous clique at her exclusive Westchester middle school when LBR (Loser Beyond Repair) Claire Lyons moves into the Blocks' guesthouse and turns Massie's perfect world upside down.

BEST FRIENDS FOR NEVER

A bet between ringleader Massie and wannabe Claire tests both their willpowers—and transforms the Octavian Country Day student body. Or at least the most important part: their wardrobes.

REVENGE OF THE WANNABES

When Alicia tries to start a clique of her own, allegiances are tested and Massie launches an all-out war—during their *Teen Vogue* photo shoot! The Pretty Committee definitely isn't ready for its close-up. . . .

INVASION OF THE BOY SNATCHERS

While the guesthouse is being renovated, Claire moves into Massie's room. But Claire isn't the only person moving into Massie's territory—Alicia's hot cousin Nina arrives from Spain and starts cozying up to all the Briarwood boys, including Massie's crush!

THE PRETTY COMMITTEE STRIKES BACK

The girls of OCD are off to Lake Placid for Presidents' Day, and with the Briarwood boys staying just a few cabins away, the girls in Massie's Underground Clinic for Kissing (MUCK) might have to put their money where their well-glossed mouths are.

DIAL L FOR LOSER

The Clique is *this close* to begging Principal Burns to readmit them to OCD when movie director Rupert Mann invites the girls to audition for his new teen blockbuster, *Dial L for Loser*. Massie thinks she's got the lead in the bag, but what happens when Claire snags the starring role?

IT'S NOT EASY BEING MEAN

The Clique is back at Octavian Country Day and they've got a new goal: finding the key that unlocks the school's legendary secret room. Alpha eighth grader Skye Hamilton has stashed the key in the bedroom of a mystery Briarwood boy—but which one? Looks like the Clique will have to search them all!

And keep your eye out for the eighth novel,
SEALED WITH A DISS, coming August 2007.

THE A-LIST

When good girl Anna Percy heads to Los Angeles to live with her dad, she quickly meets dangerously handsome Ben Birnbaum. Suddenly, Anna finds herself thrown into the wild world of Beverly Hills High—and directly in the path of the rich and catty girls who rule it.

GIRLS ON FILM

Anna heads to chic spa Veronique s with her former nemesis Sam Sharpe, but will a hot steam bath be enough to make her forget about the even hotter Ben Birnbaum?

BLONDE AMBITION

Anna's an intern on the new hit TV show *Hermosa Beach* and suddenly everyone wants to be her NBF. Everyone except for Cammie Shepard—who's not used to sharing the spotlight and will do anything to get it back.

TALL COOL ONE

Anna and Sam make a getaway to Las Casitas, Mexico, where Angelenos go to work on their tans. It doesn't take long for the girls to find a few cute guys—and a whole lot of trouble!

BACK IN BLACK

Anna and her friends head to Vegas for a glamorous three-day vacation. When they visit a hypnotist-to-the-stars and reveal their deepest, darkest secrets, the crew learns firsthand why Vegas is called Sin City!

SOME LIKE IT HOT

Ben is back for the summer—just in time to be Anna's prom date. But will his family's smokin' houseguest burn up their perfect plans?

AMERICAN BEAUTY

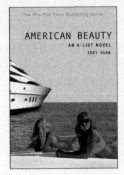

It's graduation time for the A-List, which means lavish yacht parties, designer caps and gowns, and saying bye-bye to high school . . . and hello to full-time Hollywood high life!

And keep your eye out for the eighth novel, **HEART OF GLASS**, coming April 2007.

gossip girl

After getting mysteriously kicked out of boarding school, Serena van der Woodsen is back where she belongs—Manhattan's Upper East Side, where the posh townhouses, designer clothes, and exclusive parties are almost as fabulous as she is. All eyes are on Serena, but will her former best friend Blair Waldorf be willing to share the spotlight?

you know you love me

It's Blair's seventeenth birthday, and she knows exactly what she wants—her boyfriend Nate Archibald all to herself. Too bad Blair's been too busy filling out Ivy League college applications to notice that Nate may not be a one-girl guy. . . .

all I want is everything

Blair and Serena are back to being BFFs and they're off to St. Bart's for some Christmastime fun in the sun. With a romantic rock star and a cute stepbrother in tow, it's going to be one sizzling week—on and *off* the beach!

because I'm worth it

It's Fashion Week and the only place crazier than the fashion shows are the wild parties. Will Serena's sudden catwalk stardom make her new boyfriend seem totally last season?

I like it like that

It's spring break and the whole crew is heading to Sun Valley for some après-ski hot tub fun. With Nate playing knight-in-shining-armor to his crazy new girlfriend, Georgie, and Blair batting her eyelashes at Serena's brother Erik, the nights will be hot enough to stave off the mountain cold.

you're the one that I want

Mailboxes all over the Upper East Side are piling up with overstuffed envelopes from the Ivy League. Will who-got-in-where distract people from the more important question: Who's hooking up with whom?

nobody does it better

Spring is here and everyone is getting out of
the house—and into the Plaza. Serena and
Jenny are partying in the penthouse with New
York's hippest band, The Raves, while Blair's
taken up residence to get some alone time
with Nate. And if posh hotel suites aren't
plush enough, there's always Senior Spa Day!

nothing can keep us together

When Blair and Serena go head-to-head for
the starring role in a major Hollywood
movie, there's sure to be some drama worthy
of the silver screen!

only in your dreams

It's the last summer before college, and love is
in the air. Blair's off to London with her new
British boyfriend—who's an awful lot like
Nate. Nate's smooching beach babe Tawny—
who's basically the anti-Blair. And Serena is
half of Hollywood's hot new pairing—as if she
wasn't smoldering on her own!

would I lie to you

Serena and Blair head to the Hamptons to be resident co-muses to the super-famous designer Bailey Winter, who just happens to live next door to Nate's beachside estate. So just how neighborly will these new neighbors get?

And keep your eye out for the eleventh novel, don't you forget about me, coming May 2007.

Read all the novels in the *New York Times* bestselling series

the it girl

the it girl

Popular Gossip Girl character Jenny Humphrey is leaving Constance Billard to attend elite boarding school Waverly Academy, where the rich and glamorous students don't let the rules get in the way of an excellent time.

notorious

After a wild first week at boarding school, the Waverly student body can't help but whisper about Jenny and *her* body. But after getting expelled last year, the notorious Tinsley Carmichael is back, and she's not about to let some big-chested, rosy-cheeked city girl get all the attention. After all, there can only be *one* it girl.

reckless

The girls' dorm is put on lockdown, and being stuck in close quarters isn't helping ease the tension between Jenny, Callie, Brett, and Tinsley. Will the boys find a way to sneak in and party before the girls scratch one another's MAC mad eyes out?

And keep your eye out for the fourth novel, **unforgettable**, coming June 2007.